Robert

KNIGHT WITH
No
SHIELD

A novel by

Robert J McCaldon

Special thanks to: Jane McCaldon for her understanding and classical acumen.

Barbara Jones for her Editor's eagle eye.

SUSAN RADFORD for the cover art of the Royal Military College at Kingston.

Although the conflict is contemporary reality, the plot and characters are fictional.

ISBN: 1499381875
ISBN 13: 9781499381870

Library of Congress Control Number: 2014908856
CreateSpace Independent Publishing Platform
North Charleston, South Carolina

www.RESILIENCEPUBLISHING.com

CHAPTER ONE

New York, 2001

The day was perfect for blue birds. The odd wisp of cirrus clouds adorned the azure sky above. The café, elegant yet practical, catered to important people with important jobs who stopped here for a snack and a coffee before going on to whatever it was they did for a living. Tanya Amyotte, not yet seventeen years old, knew she had arrived.

It was not merely a fluke of fate that had brought her to this place of vibrancy and hope. Although she had good genes and an understanding far above her years, it was through supreme effort of will that she'd entered this urban dynamo.

Tanya, as she was known, for all models gave out only their first name, had been a super-sensitive child. This drove her parents to exasperation, her father especially. He was a cop – a tough guy – or had been until recently.

Her mother, Noreen, though of sturdy Northern Quebec extraction too, was more in tune with feelings; more forgiving.

A jet plane rumbled across the sky, leaving a fading contrail. Tanya wondered what Alberto was doing that took him so long. She stretched out her long legs, tanned to a golden hue, under the table in the corner booth and had another sip of the latté Alberto had brought her.

She had played him expertly to get here. Her future in a world of wealth and glamour was virtually assured. He too had ambition and drive, and the contacts she needed to reach the pinnacles of fame.

Tanya had no great illusions about him. Alberto Golondrino was certainly not his real name, though he spoke fluent Spanish as well as English, French and Arabic.

The Golondrino Group was a myriad of enterprises; hotels, spas, herbal beauty enhancement products, even a team of cosmetic plastic surgeons. The pivotal one for Tanya was the Golondrino Modeling Agency.

When Tanya was seven, her abrupt, volcanic mood swings had led her to see a child psychiatrist, who recommended medication. The pharmacy gave Noreen, her mother, the mandatory list of possible side-effects. Tanya tried one pill. It made her feel like a zombie. She threw up. Projectile vomiting it was, just like the time her father had insisted she eat her goddamn porridge. That was before anyone knew that she was gluten-sensitive. She could eat rice and potatoes and most vegetables, but wheat, barley, oats and other grain products not only upset her intestines, but precipitated the rage-reactions to erupt for no discernable reason.

Karla MacTaggart, who was Tanya's maternal Grandmother and ran a sporting-goods store after the death of her husband, suggested dance lessons and maybe a modeling course.

"Well I'm not paying for that malarkey," Tanya's father had said. He used malarkey when he was really thinking *merde*. "You know, Noreen, we're barely keeping our heads above water on my cop's salary. Besides, the kid's like a fargin' dervish. How in hell is she going to stay still long enough for them to shoot one picture, let alone a string of them? This model agency stuff is all a con-shot anyway. You pay for the photographs, for a portfolio, for teaching a kid how to walk down a runway for Crissake. And what percentage of these duped parents ever gets to see their kid make a living as a model? I'll pay for a gym membership, but not this other crap. If Karla's so goddamn keen on it for Tanya, let her foot the bill!"

Tanya remembered that there had been some subsequent discussion about how much her father was squandering on booze. The upshot was that she got to do all three – work out at a gym, take dance classes <u>and</u> modeling lessons.

The weather was still summer-like. Fall didn't arrive officially for another ten days. The café had not yet turned on the air-conditioning for the day. Tanya watched the folks going by on the sidewalk outside – black, yellow, brown and white – some with briefcases, suits and ties or pearl necklaces and fashionable business skirts, Gucci shoes and genuine Rolex watches; all with a sense of purpose and belonging.

She worried not a jot about the missed classes at school. She'd easily make them up when she got back. For Tanya was not just subject to bouts of rage and despair, she also would swing up to the pinnacles of joy, even rapture, all in the blink of an eye. By the time she arrived at puberty and began her transformation from an orthodontic caterpillar into a vivacious, transfixing butterfly, Tanya had learned how to fight through the dark moments, and ride the crests of her joy and enthusiasm with gusto, taking others with her on an exciting roller-coaster. Tanya developed a personality. Not only had she achieved poise, grace, a portfolio, she'd learned the knack of manipulating others.

She looked at her watch, with as much impatience as Alberto had before he'd gone off to take care of some business. They were due inside the sky scraper, somewhere on the twenty-first floor around ten thirty. Oh well, there was time yet. The elevators here in New York are superbly efficient, she knew.

At almost-seventeen, Tanya knew she was gorgeous, and that she had an edge with Alberto. The Agency where she'd trained had been affiliated with the Golondrino Group. A couple of felicitous jobs at the local level had caught Alberto's eye and Tanya was able to get a personal interview with him.

At first sight, she could sense the dynamism in his dark eyes. For what? For power, fame, fortune? Of course, all these. But he also had the hots for her, and that gave her an edge.

Her flirtation had been subtle; a lingering glance, a moist-lipped smile, an accidental touch of her hand on the shoulder of his silk shirt. It was easy getting invited here.

It had not been easy getting her parents to acquiesce. She didn't see much of her father in the two years since her parents separated, but she knew he was antipathetic to Alberto, whom he usually called that greasy fag. Once she obtained her mother's approval, she knew her father would agree, if only to buy a little peace at the Family Court where his support payments were being challenged constantly by Noreen.

Tanya sipped the last of her now-cold latté. The dregs of the cup had a bitter taste. Once more she resumed her game of people watching. She'd select individuals passing by the open window on the sidewalk, give them names, and conjure-up in her mind their occupations, their home life, their fears, and joys and aspirations. Most were heading into the office towers. A few were walking away.

One of these was Alberto, and he was hustling. To catch a friend before he got into a cab?

Tanya began a mental review of her ultimate strategy. She'd known that Alberto would expect a little pay-back for bringing her here to the

Big Apple as his hot, new, protégé. She was clever enough to keep him hungering for more. Satisfying him had been ridiculously easy; as easy as it had been with Bucky Adam, high school football quarterback and team captain, in the back seat of his father's Audi. She didn't even have to do the whole thing, so eager was he to get to that ultimate squirt-squirt which had to be some kind of gorgeous Nirvana for guys. Tanya had learned to satisfy herself years before and felt totally in control of these kinds of situations.

But it was what came later that was the key. She'd played coy and virginal; told Alberto she was shocked at how far she had progressed into their relationship. Yes, that's what it was to her. And in a relationship, she expected tenderness, trust, commitment and security. She casually spoke of a (fictitious) friend who had "given herself completely" to an older man, a teacher, and when rejected, she had no option but to charge him with abusing his status as mentor and teacher and exploiting her. The criminal charges ended the teacher's career. The civil suit was for six hundred thousand. Tanya thought that was a cool number. It was never paid, however, as the disgraced teacher committed suicide, so she told him.

After this bedtime story, Tanya had snuggled up to Alberto, both naked in the monstrous bed as big as half of a tennis court and said, "But I feel completely secure with you, Alberto. You are a wonderful man, and I'm grateful to you for what you have done for me and what you are teaching me. Be careful, My Love, for what you hold in your hand is my heart".

Then she'd got up, dressed quickly, and gone to her own room down the hall.

That had been last night. Now, a languor was coming over her, a delicious feeling of relaxation. Perhaps there was not enough caffeine in the latté. Where on earth was her Latin lover, Alberto? Maybe, he was arranging a runway presentation of his most glamorous gown creation, with her wearing it.

Tanya Amyotte, aspirant super-model and not yet seventeen was only vaguely aware of the jet plane coming in too low through the azure sky and exploding in the tower behind her. She slipped under the table, unnoticed and semi-conscious as the people she'd been watching came running by her, seeking escape from the suffocating black smoke and grit raining down.

Within an hour the café was buried under the rubble.

* * *

CHAPTER TWO

Northern Quebec, 1945

D enis Amyotte cursed the church, and all that was in it – the crucifix, altar, the chalice, the host. These were the worst of the curses in Canadian French, worse even than the scatological or the sexual. But he cursed mainly for a very personal reason. His wife had just told him she was pregnant again. This would be her eighth. Denis would have seven children to support, if this one lived. It probably would, for only one had died in infancy.

Denis loved them all, of course, but seven! Well, there were other couples, like the Tremblants, who had twelve, but they had no ambition to get out of this place. Denis did. That is why he worked so hard and became foreman.

Why couldn't his wife go to the English doctor, Connors, instead of that Pope-bound Dr. Turcotte? It was rumored that Dr. Connors could help women not to have too many babies. That is why Father Simard forbade his parishioners to go to that doctor. If you have plenty of children, then it was God's will, and you accept what you get from God. That's what Denis Amyotte's wife told him, worn out though she was with her role as baby-factory and mother. Denis thought such thinking was *merde*. When the priest puts a meal on my table, then maybe I listen to him, he'd told her.

A rumbling jolt moved through the bowels of the earth and shook the toilet seat where Denis was sitting. He was used to this, for he lived very close to the Nordisque Mine, where he worked underground.

He looked at his watch. If that blast was where he thought, he and his crew would have to clean out the rubble and get it hauled up to the surface. He was to start work in an hour. One hopes the dust wouldn't be so bad to add to the cough he was developing. When it was really dusty, the men would inhale aluminum powder before going below, to protect their lungs. Denis suspected that it did dick-all.

The elevator cage was full when he got there. He had to wait. It would be at least twenty minutes before he could descend to join his crew.

Climbing up a slag heap, Denis lit a cigarette, the last he'd have on his shift, and looked out over the lake. It was beautiful in summer, and con-venient in winter, for people could go onto the ice and get groceries at the new supermarket, hauling sleds or even driving the few cars that were not up on blocks for the winter. By spring, just before break-up, such journeys were a crap-shoot. Every year some foolhardy soul would break through and be lost until dredged-up later when the lake was ice-free. He gazed across to the ski slope, the municipal swimming pool and beyond that the impassive forested hills stretching out to meet the flatter taiga. Then past the tree-line, it was tundra all the way to James Bay.

"Have you heard the news, Denis?" The question was in English. Dr. James MacTaggart, Exploration Geologist, was climbing up the slag heap to join him.

"*Non*. I didn't put on my radio this morning, doctor."

"I'm just a rock doctor. You can call me James, or Jim. The news is that the War is finally over. Japan just surrendered."

"Oh, that's good news for sure, that. How come you never went, James? We French, you know, we don't mess in European Wars. But *les Anglais*? They line up to go over there and get blown to pieces. Me, I got enough chance to do that right here."

"I'm colour-blind, Denis. I can't tell brown from gray. They wouldn't take me."

Denis grinned. "You'd shoot the wrong soldier? That's why! But I bet you're glad you're here, and alive, like I am."

James MacTaggart nodded. There was a pause.

"Is your crew working in Shaft Number Seven?"

"*Oui*. That's where. I miss the last cage. Have to catch the next."

"Do you mind if I go down there with you, Denis?"

Amyotte's eyes widened in surprise. It wasn't often that the top geologist would go down below. Core samples and ore were better seen in daylight. MacTaggart must know something. "Oh sure. We get over there now. I show you what we got down in Seven."

After the rapid descent, which flipped their stomachs and threatened to rupture their eardrums, Denis Amyotte showed James MacTaggart the ore that was coming out of Shaft Number Seven. There were veins of nickel and copper of course, but something else. Both men saw it, and knew immediately what it was.

MacTaggart carefully pocketed one piece, about the size of a pine cone. "Denis, I'd like you to shut down work on this shaft for now. Take your crew over to Number Nine. And *gardez la bouche*, Denis. There could be a promotion waiting for you when I get back."

"A promotion. My, that be nice. Hardly any French get higher than foreman, James. You can do this for me?'

"I'll certainly see what I can do."

"You can count on me, Doctor," said Denis Amyotte.

* * *

Karla MacTaggart skipped by the garbage wagon, which was drawn by horses. Her friend, Evelyn Lam, stopped to stroke the soft muzzle of one of them. "Does he bite?" she asked the driver in French.

"No, but I wouldn't trust the other one. Get along, now girls, I have work to do."

They were in the alley, which ran behind all the houses. The alley was for delivery of ice, coal, food, and for garbage collection. Horses provided the tractor-power, summer and winter. The two girls, both eight years old, were coming home from school.

"Your French is better than mine, Evelyn. Why do you go to the English School?"

"My parents say they have the best teachers, and you don't have to be a Catholic to go there. We Chinese pick-up the local language wherever we find ourselves. I already know how to talk Cantonese and Mandarin, and read, too. French and English are easy compared to them."

"Oh, Evelyn, I love hearing your parents talk. It's so...so...you won't feel bad if I say it sounds funny?"

"It doesn't sound funny to me. But if you like, you can come over to our place. My Mom said you could, and she has some Chinese fortune cookies for us, and sweet tea. You can smile if you like, but promise not to laugh when we talk Chinese. I know it is almost like singing, but the tone is important in understanding the words."

"I won't laugh. You're my best friend, Evelyn. I can't stay for long though. My Mom would get worried."

Mrs. Lam welcomed the two girls effusively, and fussed over Karla as though she were an English princess.

They sat in the kitchen of the Chinese restaurant, owned by the Lams, who also had a laundry that was adjacent. The kitchen was full of wonderful aromas. Mr. Lam was busy cooking, and beamed at the girls as he did so, in between giving orders to Evelyn's older brother, who also helped in the kitchen. Two other girls, both cousins of Evelyn, worked as waitresses.

"Your father, he make big train ride to Toronto?" Mrs. Lam asked. She pronounced it "Tolonto."

Karla was surprised for just a second, then not so. Her Dad had run to catch the train in his work shirt and mining boots and marched into head office with the chunk of gold ore. The bosses were very excited.

"Yes. He came back yesterday," Karla replied.

"He happy? Evleybody happy?"

Karla knew she was not to mention the truth, not to anybody. "Oh yes. He's always happy. He's a happy father." She munched the last of her fortune cookie. Her fortune said "Be true to your friends, and good luck will follow you."

Mrs. Lam said something to Evelyn in Chinese.

Karla didn't laugh. The tone was pleasant enough, but there was a serious look in those oriental eyes.

"Let's go," Evelyn said. "Mom says you'd like to see my Chinese doll collection."

The two girls went out the back into the alley, then past the laundry, and climbed up a few wooden steps to the dwelling of the Lams.

As Karla looked at the "collection" of three dolls in Evelyn's room, she began to cry.

"What's wrong? Don't you like my dolls?"

"Yes. They're beautiful. I just…I just didn't know." Karla gestured vaguely at the cracked window, the thin walls where the winter wind would creep in through the crevices and freeze the flesh, the sagging bed, the worn mat on the floor, and the chamber pot beside it.

"Where is your bathroom?" Karla asked

"Down the hall. Three families share it." Evelyn hung her head. "I can't help it, Karla. This is where I live. We Chinese came here with nothing. But we're smart, and we work hard and spend little. When I have kids, they'll live in a palace; a palace like the King and Queen." Tears were filling her eyes too.

Suddenly, Karla sensed what Mrs. Lam was after. She didn't know how it would help, but if she could, she'd tell the secret to her best friend.

"What my Dad found was gold, Evelyn. Lots of it. If you tell your Mom this, just be sure you don't say it came from me. Say it was from one of the Amyotte boys. Their Dad is a miner, and sometimes he drinks too much and lets slip things that are secrets. Promise me, Evelyn?"

"I promise," she said, and hugged her. Then she gave Karla one of her precious Chinese dolls.

* * *

Denis Amyotte did drink too much, but this secret he guarded carefully, waiting to see how Nordisque Mines would treat him.

They gave him a supervisory job up top. The pay was better and he wouldn't have to go down that *maudite* mine again.

Just before moose hunting season, he went into the office of James MacTaggart, who was often away from this mine, working with survey crews, seismic drilling projects, and talking with freelance prospectors.

Today MacTaggart was in his office. Amyotte wanted a week off to go moose hunting.

"Of course, Denis. Take more if you want. How is the new job going?'

"Very good. James I thank you for what you done for me. If you invest fast in this mine, you could get rich, you, *non?*"

"It's not allowed, Denis. It's called Insider Trading. <u>You</u> can't do it either."

"Your wife – could she do it?"

"Maybe. It would be better if someone with a different name were to invest. Besides, this vein could run out at any time, and then the stocks would crash."

"But in the meantime, the smart thing to do is buy low and sell high. And it will go high when word gets around, *n'est ce pas?*"

"That's a sound business principle, Denis."

"James, would you loan me ten thousand dollars? We get it drawn up all legal. I pay you twelve percent interest annually. Probably I pay it all back within a year – two tops. I give the fund to my cousin who invest for me. We'll call it Marcel Avenir. That's his name, Marcel. What you say? I got to move fast on this, for it to work."

"I don't have ten thousand."

"But you can get it! Tell the bank you need to do home renovations. They'll lend it to you at six percent. I'll give you twelve. How can you lose?"

MacTaggart hesitated.

"My wife, she's in the family way again. I want to make a better life for my seven kids than I ever had."

MacTaggart could sense the desperation. He could help this man. "It's a deal."

There were four profiteers from the discovery of gold – the MacTaggarts, the Amyottes, the Lams, and, of course Nordisque Mines and all its investors.

* * *

CHAPTER THREE

Kingston, Ontario. 2001

Rick Amyotte arose late, fumbled about in the bedroom and then the bathroom for his packet of nicotine patches, and, in frustration, lit a cigarette, the last one he had. The first jolt woke him up, made him feel almost human again. "This is good; this can't hurt me", his instinctive brain said. His forebrain broke in with, "Stupid, this will kill you, just as surely as it did your father".

As he shaved and stood under a shower, Rick tried to piece together the events of last night. They were patchy, fragmented as in a dream. As he dressed, he saw the half-empty bottle of Glenfiddich scotch. Yesterday, when he left, it had been full. The glass beside it had made yet another ring in the finish of the wooden bedside table. He'd swilled down thirteen ounces of scotch on top of what he had already consumed in the bar!

The Glenfiddich had been a gift from his middle-aged student at the Kingston Trap, Skeet and Sporting Clays Club, also known as the Italian-Canadian Club. Rick was a member, and the management let him give private lessons in shotgunning for the cost of the targets plus twenty-five dollars. Rick charged one hundred bucks an hour. It had been a three-hour lesson.

He also belonged to the nearby Frontenac Rifle and Pistol Club, for he taught the Firearms and Hunter Safety Training courses there. The Italian Club didn't have rifle and pistol; the Frontenac Club didn't have shotgun. Between the two sites, Rick was barely able to make a living, though Noreen's ceaseless demands through the Family Court kept him rather impecunious. Life had definitely taken a nosedive since he'd lost his job as a cop, and had been forced out of his own house.

He frowned. Had he put the shotguns away in the metal safe? There were only two closets in his tiny bungalow on a gravel road south of Verona – not the one in Italy, the one in Frontenac County, Ontario. One closet had all of his clothes for summer and winter. The other had all of his firearms and ammo, the real ones in a gun safe, the training guns loosely stacked, disabled, with a yellow plastic piece of tape around the barrel and stored with the dummy ammo in the various calibres and gauges that he used for training.

He found the shotguns where they should be, in the safe. Some habits can be good, he mused.

Pulling back the curtains, Rick saw the sun trying to dry the dew on the shady side of his bungalow. The dwelling had no cellar, for it was built on the lowlands near a vast swamp stretching to the west. The mosquitoes were a bitch in spring and summer, but now they, and the voracious deer flies, were all fading fast as autumn approached.

Rick owned a much-patched fiberglass canoe, once red but now spritzed with camo paint in tan and green. Two hundred metres from his back door, there was a natural channel, made by beavers and muskrats. It wasn't his property, nor even his landlord's, but he'd hacked a path through the brush to the channel and intended to spend the rest of the day making a duck blind in the small open area he'd discovered last winter when he'd trudged back there on the ice.

The migratory bird season started in two weeks. If he fed the pond with a bag of corn right now, and if the ducks found it and cleaned it up, they might still be there on opening morning looking hopeful, and he might have a half-hour of good shooting before they wised-up.

A lot of ifs, he thought, just like the rest of his life. He recalled his father's expression; "If the dog hadn't stopped for a shit, he'd have caught the rabbit." He'd said it in French. It was a German expression he'd learned from one of the supervisors at the Nordisque Mines. Rick knew nothing about that place except what he'd been told by his parents, for they'd moved to Southern Ontario from Northern Québec when he was five years old.

Well, his dad had acted incisively then, investing shrewdly in the mines that he knew were worthy. Then, once retired and comfortable, he'd snatched failure from the jaws of success. He'd drank and smoked himself to death. Rick thought it was defiance against his mother's sanctimonious nattering. Compulsive defiance could be just as neurotic as compulsive compliance. He'd read that in a Psychology Today magazine.

Rick Amyotte thought about breakfast and decided he couldn't quite face it yet. He went into the bathroom and brushed his teeth.

What was her name? Sherri. Twenty-something, a red-head with freckles. She'd been close to tears at the bar in The Hub, Kingston's most notorious night-life scene, when Rick picked her up. He was there for that very purpose. Sherri's boyfriend was making out on the dance floor with another chick and would probably take the new one home. This made Sherri vulnerable to Rick's knight-to-rescue-fair-damsel routine.

"Rick," she'd said when he introduced himself and offered to buy her a drink. "Is that short for Richard?"

"Yes, except when I was a kid, it was pronounced the French way, Reeshar. Don't call me Ricky, it sounds like I'm thirteen years old. Dick is totally not an option. I have one; I don't want to be one. So call me Rick."

She giggled. "Okay Rick. You can buy me a Vodka Screw Driver. I like the name of that drink."

"So do I," Rick said, and knew he was going to score.

Sherri's apartment was within walking distance of The Hub. They were both rather relaxed and rubbery when they got there. A few pulls on a toke relaxed them more.

For Sherri, this encounter was yet another vain hope for abiding love. For Rick, it was any port in a storm.

At five in the morning, after he'd slept-off the worst of the night's booze, he quietly got out of bed, dressed, went out to find his car, and drove home. At that hour, it only took forty minutes. But why in hell did he then get into the scotch?

He was just putting on the coffee when the telephone rang. The call display told him it was Noreen, probably wanting more money, "for Tanya's career." He hesitated, not sure he wanted to deal with her before he got at least one cup of black coffee into his queasy stomach. The answering service would kick in at five rings. He grabbed the receiver at four.

"Yeah. What now?"

"Rick, turn on your T.V., any channel."

Noreen's voice was tremulous. "Stay on the line. But turn on the goddamn T.V!"

Rick laid the phone down, rummaged around for the remote control, found it and hit the power button.

The volume was too low to hear what the announcer was saying. When the image came, it was of a jet liner crashing into one of the Twin Towers of the World Trade Center in New York.

Rick snatched up the telephone again. "Have you heard from her? Is she all right?"

"So far, there's no word. And nothing yet from the Golondrino Group. Rick, I know you're no longer a cop, but could you find out...something?" Maybe Milos could get in touch with the New York Police. Would you ask him? We have to find out!"

"Yeah. I'll see what I can do. Stay home for the next couple of hours. I'll call you if I get anything. I knew we shouldn't have let that greasy spik put Tanya in harm's way!"

"Alberto couldn't know. Who could do such a thing?"

Rick upped the volume on the T.V. in time to learn that another aircraft had hit the second tower. The Pentagon in Washington was struck by another plane, and one more jet liner was missing. The announcer was speculating about White Supremacists, like Timothy McVeigh, the Oklahoma City Bomber.

"Idiot!" Rick screamed at the television, and also into the phone.

"Who?" Noreen asked.

"The announcer. It's exactly what Osama bin Laden said he'd do, except nobody wanted to believe him. It's the current source of most of the disasters in the world – camel-loving, rag-head, Muslim, fucking terrorists! Noreen, I'll see what I can find out."

As Rick Amyotte punched in the number of his ex-partner in the Ontario Provincial Police, Sergeant Milos Novak, he looked out the window. The day was still bright and sunny, but now a malignant dread seemed to lurk in the dark shadows of autumn.

* * *

CHAPTER FOUR

The opening day of the migratory bird season did not dawn with Rick Amyotte with a shotgun, crouched in a canoe in his secret pond. Instead, he was on a flight to New York with his estranged wife, Noreen.

Security at Toronto's Pearson Airport was tight. When they landed in New York, it was like the defense of the Alamo. Armed soldiers with assault rifles at the ready stood alert every fifty metres, and in between these were police and security guards.

Rick and Noreen had sat together on the plane, but said little. They were united in grief, but the animosity seethed just under the veneer of forced politeness. When Rick ordered a scotch from the flight attendant, Noreen sighted audibly before asking for tomato juice.

At the morgue, there was no longer any doubt. Milos Novak had warned them in advance, but human nature being what it is, they both clung to a shred of hope that somehow, Tanya had gotten away.

The body had been found, somewhat crushed and mutilated, together with her purse, on the eleventh of September. This was the only corpse in the former café, except for a male oriental cook who had inexplicably locked himself in the bathroom. All the others had fled in time, including Alberto Golondrino.

On the twelfth, Golondrino had telephoned each parent separately, expressing his regret and sorrow. He'd lost not only Tanya, but three other friends and employees of his model agency. It was only a chance meeting that had drawn him out of the café and into the street before the crash. He'd tried to run back in to save Tanya, but police and firemen blocked his path and eventually dragged him away protesting, so he said.

"They told me, 'Let us handle this, sir. We're trained to do this.' The smoke was thick, suffocating. Even with oxygen masks, they couldn't go back there. I am so sorry. She was like a daughter to me."

On the plane, Rick and Noreen learned that he'd used almost the exact same words to each of them.

As they stared down at the charred mass of flesh that had been their daughter, they could see the faint scar under her left ear where she'd fallen off her bike on her first solo ride and tore open the skin on a rose bush. The necklace, a light chain of Taxco silver that they had given Tanya on her fifteenth birthday, was still around the scorched neck. They asked the attendant to turn over the body, and there was the purple and green butterfly tattoo at the base of her spine. No, there was no longer any doubt.

"If you want to be sure," the attendant said, "we can arrange for DNA testing. It would take a week and cost you three thousand dollars."

They both shook their heads. "Let's just ship her home," Rick muttered.

As they left the morgue, Rick almost collided with an Arab man in a long, white, hooded burnouse. Instead of the usual self-effacing "Pardon me," typical of Canadians, Rick just glared at him.

The hatred shot like voltage between the two men for a second.

Noreen tugged on Rick's arm to get him away. "He didn't do it. Why blame him?" she whispered when they were a few steps away.

"He didn't stop it either. Fucking rag-head. It's a religion of hatred, striving for world domination."

"No...no! Islam is a religion of peace. Most Muslims are decent folks."

"When Adolph Hitler first came to power, most Germans weren't Nazis, and look what he did, when no one stood up to oppose him. Where is the Muslim condemnation? Most of them think the Jews and George Bush secretly planned this atrocity. Improbable as it seems, Israel has to be culpable somehow, in their twisted logic. It's a Middle East democracy, and they can't abide that."

"Let's not argue. Let's just get Tanya home and buried."

"I need a drink," Rick muttered.

* * *

CHAPTER FIVE

"I can't do it, Rick," Milos Novak said. "It's not like the old days, Man. Now, if you want something tracked, you gotta do a ton of paper work. It's just a match box with a phone number scribbled on it. Probably just the number of a friend."

"And a set of initials, 'DG.' Does that ring any bells?" Rick demanded.

"No, not immediately." Novak shifted his gaze down to his massive hands that were folded on his desk. He was not in uniform now, for he worked with the OPP Pen Squad, the police investigation unit for crimes occurring within the seven federal penitentiaries in the Kingston area.

"Is Dieter Gipfel still inside?"

"Oh. You think maybe DG means him?"

"Milos, don't play dumb, goddamn it! Is that little Kraut shit still inside? You'd know if anyone would."

"Last I heard he was in Bath Institution. Ideal inmate there, polite, obedient. I'll check for you."

When Milos reached for the telephone, Rick could see a flash of silver and emerald cufflinks. Milos had seemingly done well in the two years since they were partners in the South Frontenac Detachment.

When he got off the telephone, he shook his head. "No, Dieter Gipfel got paroled four months ago. Address is listed as Belleville. The number you have is a Kingston exchange."

"And Belleville is only an hour's drive from Kingston."

"Rick, let it be. Nothing you can do will bring her back. Don't torture yourself. Bury your daughter, and get on with your life."

"It's because of that schmuck that I lost my job!"

"No, Rick. Your boozing played a major part too." Milos held up his hands when he saw Rick's reaction.

"No, no, what they did to you wasn't right, Man. I tried to get them to drop it, but shots were fired, and someone got injured."

"Yeah, and it just had to be a member of a visible minority; a Muslim woman. I didn't shoot her. Dieter Gipfel did!"

"Well, he did time for it. You didn't."

"I just lost my job – my career."

"Yeah. It's tough. Maybe if I'd been with you that night, things would have worked out differently. But I was stuck in a snow-bank. That's why they asked you to investigate the disturbance – work a double shift. Most of the rest of us were either snow-bound or unsnarling fender-benders and checking cars in ditches."

"I'm not blaming you, Milos," Rick sighed. "I did have a drink or two that night, thinking I would remain safe at home. The call to come in and work a double was a surprise. But I wasn't pissed. When I went into that mansion, nobody was threatening nobody with any gun. Klaus Gipfel, the old man, had the Colt Trooper out on his work-bench, cleaning it when his stoned son had come in by snow-mobile and began raggin' at the father for more cash. It was Klaus who put in the call, to get that disruptive prick safely removed before something bad happened.

"I thought I had everyone calmed down, before I left. You know how it is. The sight of a uniform usually makes folks mild as kittens. It was snowing heavily, and I was worried I wouldn't be able to make it out the road from Fourteen Island Lake. You've been there. It has more twists than a python.

"So I left the two of them together, and I did not confiscate the gun. Gipfel Senior has always been a responsible gun owner. How was I to know that Junior would wait until his father was asleep, grab the gun and ammo and go shoot up a pharmacy, looking for cash and Dilaudid? And the pharmacist, Miryam Tomari, blamed me for not securing the gun and blamed me more than the guy who shot her! How's that for justice? Heads had to roll to appease the politically correct minions of our grand multicultural society."

"Very eloquent, Rick. Justice is blind, and sometimes she's a bitch. Miryam's husband, Omar Tomari, also a pharmacist, tried to keep her from making a formal complaint against you. But she said she smelled booze on you when you went to investigate. And she was lying there, bleeding, with a .357 Magnum slug through her thigh. They had to take her complaint seriously. Sharia law condemns alcohol, Rick. She's a fanatic. Her husband's not. And they've sold the pharmacy in Sydenham and are now running a Pharmaceutical distribution warehouse, near Napanee, west of Kingston. Doing quite well. She still walks with a limp though."

"I need a drink." Rick said. He picked up the match box with the telephone number and was about to leave.

"Rick? When and where is the memorial service?"

"Day after tomorrow. Collin's Bay United Church. Two P.M."

"I'll be there."

"Thanks, Milos."

* * *

It is a criminal offense to impersonate a police officer. Rick doubted that anyone cared though, that he'd extracted the address to which the phone number belonged from Bell Telephone, posing as a cop. The house was on Cherry Street, north of Princess. The owner was an I. Ghali, who must be slumming, if the silver Mercedes parked in the driveway belonged to him or her.

On the street, a maroon Dodge Durango, 4X4 was parked. The license plate read "SCOOTER". The raindrops beaded in glistening puddles on the fresh wax job. Royal purple, how classy, Rick thought as he sat in his car a couple of houses down, and waited.

Two men appeared on the porch, shook hands, and took off in their separate vehicles. The Mercedes belonged to Alberto Golondrino.

The Durango with the SCOOTER plate was driven by Dieter Gipfel. Prison life must have agreed with him. He was still squat and dark, a sneaky troll, but he'd put on weight, some of it muscle, and obviously had amassed some cash.

This business wasn't about the model agency, or cosmetic creams. The whole scenario screamed of drugs.

* * *

Kingston General Hospital overlooks that part of Lake Ontario as it is turning into the St. Lawrence River; the beginning of the Thousand Islands, of salad dressing fame, though most folks don't know why. Lucky patients get a view of the Lake, of the Martello Tower built to protect Kingston from American attack, and of Wolfe Island beyond, named after the General who defeated Montcalm on the Plains of Abraham at Quebec

City. This established British supremacy in Canada from that day forth, but someone forgot to tell the French.

The Toxicology Department did not overlook Lake Ontario. It was in the basement of the Hospital.

The head honcho was a Chinese woman, not quite forty, slender figure and a no-nonsense gaze. "What, exactly is it you're asking me to do, Sergeant Amyotte?" she asked him.

"Ex-Sergeant. Call me Rick, Doctor."

"If you'll call me Lucy." There was a mischievous smile at the corners of her mouth.

Rick told her.

Lucy wasn't terribly enthusiastic, but agreed.

They shook hands on it.

"When and where is the memorial service, Rick?" she asked.

He told her, as he had Milos Novak. "Did you ever meet Tanya, Lucy?"

"No. But her grandmother and my mother were best friends in Northern Quebec. I'd like to pay my respects. I feel like I sort of knew her."

Rick looked at her name tag for the first time.

Dr. Lucy Lam, it said.

* * *

Noreen was furious with Rick for postponing the cremation. She had the backing of Milos Novak. "Forget about it, Rick. You're grasping at straws. There's nothing there," he insisted. They were outside the United Church in Collin's Bay, now part of Kingston.

"Besides," Noreen said, "it's a further desecration of our daughter's corpse."

"Look, we can still have the Service. Right now. All that's different is that Tanya's body will be cremated a day later. The test won't involve a full autopsy. They already did a quick post-mortem in New York. I just need some tissue samples for toxicology studies."

Noreen agreed, "Only if it will make you go away and stop interfering, Rick, as you always do."

Milos tried to persuade her otherwise, but she waved him away.

"Who is doing the investigation? That Oriental ghoul you met, Rick?" Noreen asked.

Karla MacTaggart, Noreen's mother, who'd been silent until then, spoke up. "That Oriental ghoul just happens to be the daughter of Evelyn Lam, my best childhood friend in Quebec. If she thinks it's worthwhile doing, then do it."

And that was that.

* * *

It was the first of October, with the leaves a riot of crimson and gold, when Lucy Lam telephoned Rick at his home north of Verona.

"There are high levels of Ketamine Hydrochloride in liver, kidneys and brain, Rick.

"Ketamine?"

"It's one of the date rape drugs. It's used as a general anesthetic Low doses disinhibit; puts one into a dissociative state. High doses can render one unconscious, unable to function. Muscles and respiration are maintained, but awareness of what's going on is grossly impaired. Tanya couldn't flee.

"Tanya died of asphyxiation, though, didn't she…?"

"Yes, of course. But she likely would have gotten out of there if she hadn't been toxic with this stuff. And if it wasn't taken voluntarily, which

28

might be difficult to prove, then it's probably technically a homicide – manslaughter or murder. What do you want me to do about this, Rick?"

* * *

CHAPTER SIX

As his vehicle eased around the end of a wooded swamp, three Canada geese took off, honking raucously. Two were fully grown, one was smaller. Rick wondered what had become of the rest of the brood. Then he spied a pair of gray ospreys gliding over the swamp. That must be it. Avian predation. Ospreys eat mainly frogs and fish, but like most predators, they are opportunists and would take off with a fledgling gosling in their rapacious talons in an eye blink.

As he rounded the next curve of the gravel road, a red fox darted in front of his right fender and into a crimson sumac bush, flaming in the morning sunlight. The sumacs would be a good place to hunt for ruffed grouse, known locally as partridge.

The road, sinuous and hilly, wound its way down to the rocky shore of Fourteen Island Lake. Rick Amyotte was on his way to talk with Klaus Gipfel, father of Dietrich, or Dieter as he was called.

Rick had told Dr. Lucy Lam to file her report about the Ketamine found in Tanya's body in the usual way, but not to be in too big a hurry to bring it to police attention. If it could be proven that a crime was committed, it was committed in New York. The NYPD had their hands full of investigations and body recoveries, with many sick officers off duty because of toxic smoke inhalation. They wouldn't welcome the Canadian constabulary to complicate their lives. Rick wanted to do a bit of investigative work on his own – connect the dots, as he used to say to Milos.

He hadn't been down Deer Park Lane since that snowy night he'd left Dieter and his father in the mansion, with the Colt Trooper .357 Magnum lying out on the work-bench where Klaus had been cleaning it. How was he to know the drug-addicted sneak would go and shoot Miryam Tomari in the leg? And later, when he went to give her first aid on the floor of the pharmacy in Sydenham, when she smelled the whisky on his breath, how could she blame him for the shooting? Hell, he'd only had a couple of drinks that night. It wasn't as though he was drunk on the job!

The pines which surrounded the mansion stood like green sentinels behind the high, chain link fence, all framed by scarlet maples, golden and white birches and wine-dark oaks. Stopping the car, he absent-mindedly reached to his shirt pocket for a cigarette until he remembered that he'd quit…again. Praise be to the patch. It makes it bearable. Now if they only had a patch for alcoholics…

As he exited his car, a grouse thundered off from the gravel by the intercom box. The grouse sat in a pine tree behind the fence, mocking him as he pushed the button.

"Yes?" the voice crackled.

"It's Rick Amyotte. I called earlier, Mr. Gipfel."

"Ah, yes. Drive in. Please shut the gate after you."

The lock clacked open audibly and the gate retracted by gravity, because of the slight angle of the steel post on which it hung. Rick imagined that there would be generator back-up in case of a power failure. Gipfel Senior seemed very well organized.

As he parked his car by the main dwelling, Rick heard dogs barking. By the large red-brick kennel, a ferocious German Shepherd showed his fangs. A more docile Weimaraner bitch, the German gray ghost, gave a ritual yap or two, but was more curious than resentful.

The man himself was there to welcome him at the front door. Klaus Gipfel was tall, erect, with a gray mustache and goatee, wearing military surplus eight-pocket pants, ankle-high hiking boots and a tan shirt with button shoulder-straps.

Germans all love uniforms, Rick thought as they shook hands.

The den where they sat was paneled with rich, dark wood. Antlers of various animals dotted the walls. A boar skin rug lay on the parquet hardwood. It looked like it came from a five hundred pounder. A stuffed drake wood-duck formed the base of a lamp. Gipfel turned on the lamp, though a skylight above gave plenty of light to the room.

"How can I help you, Sergeant?" he asked.

"I'm not a Sergeant. I was. Now I'm retired from the Force. This is a personal call, Mr.Gipfel."

"Call me Klaus."

"Okay. Call me Rick. I'm here to talk with you about your son, Dieter."

"He was in jail. He's out now. I hope he's learned something in the process. That's all I can say. I don't see much of him now, after what... after his arrest." He was silent after that, waiting.

Rick looked around the room again. "You're a hunter, Klaus. It appears you are a good one."

"I've had some luck at times. A few good shots make up for all the dumb misses. But I'm not a hunter now. I lost all my guns after Dieter's transgression. They're stored with a friend, but I'm legally constrained from touching them for another three months, and then I have to take a fresh firearms course." His steely gray eyes bored bitterly into Rick's.

"Yeah. It's tough. I should have had you lock up that handgun that night; maybe taken Dieter into custody. I'm sorry, Klaus, that things turned out the way they did for you."

Klaus relaxed perceptibly. "I don't blame you. It's just how circumstances fit together, like a string of pearls. In this case, black pearls. I tried, with the boy, to bring him up right, but I failed. Maybe prison will straighten him out, but I'm not optimistic. His mother, my ex-wife, always spoiled him, as did her mother. They never experienced what I lived through. They saw a too-comfortable reality. There were never any consequences for Dieter's failings, and never any demands made on him. No discipline. Of course, it was over him that we broke-up."

"You grew up in post-war Germany?"

"The Eastern Sector. Under the Russians. In 1945 I was four years old, huddled and half-starving under a stairway, while my mother was being raped by a Russian soldier. Fortunately, my paternal grandparents had a farm and my mother sent me there in '47. At least there was something to eat. And they saw to it that I got a half-decent education."

"You're an engineer of some type, aren't you?"

"No. I studied sciences and technology and my first job was as a lens grinder. This trade came in handy when I eluded the Stasi – the secret police – and escaped to the West. I never did get an engineering degree."

"When did you come to Canada?"

"In 1959. Rick, I'm so old I remember when gay meant carefree and happy, pot was something you made tea in and rap meant the penalty for a crime."

"And a mouse ate cheese, a fire-wall stopped your house from burning down and a hacker was a lousy golfer," Rick added. "It looks to me as though you've done very well here, Klaus. Summit Industries is your company. It's mainly into optics?"

Klaus nodded, "Cameras, microscopes, telescopes, and some high-tech military stuff that has proven very lucrative. My name, Gipfel, means peak or summit in German. The company is doing very well, and it didn't just happen by chance. It took twenty years of eighteen-hour days to bring it to where it is today. But wealth doesn't mend a broken heart, my friend."

Rick thought of Tanya and winced. He changed the subject. "That Weimaraner you have…what's her name?"

"How observant of you, Rick! Most Canadians can't tell the difference between a Weimaraner, a Vizla or a Pudel-pointer. Her name is Treu." He pronounced it "Troy."

"True or faithful, as in `Der Treu Hussar.´ The first time I went grouse hunting was with a German friend who had a Weimaraner named Treu. I'll bet she misses the hunting."

"You bet correctly," Klaus said dryly. "I miss being out with her but you still haven't told me the purpose of your visit, Rick."

"Will you be here tomorrow?"

"I could be."

"I have a 20 gauge Belgian Browning Superposed that just might fit you. And I suspect there are a few grouse in the thickets around here. Let's take Treu hunting!"

Klaus was beaming. "I won't be in trouble with this?"

"No, you'll be with me. I'm a Firearms Instructor. We're just starting your mandatory course a bit early. The local Conservation Officer's a friend of mine. Do you still have your Outdoor Card?"

"*Jawohl*! It's good for one more year. Is this really why you came here, Rick – to take me and Treu hunting?"

"No, but it suddenly seems like a splendid idea, Klaus, *nicht wahr?*"

* * *

CHAPTER SEVEN

After World War One, some German aristocrats who were avid hunters founded a club to develop a new breed of hunting dog. They wanted a universal hunter that would track, point, retrieve from land or water and be intelligent, loyal and trainable. They cross bred hounds, retrievers and pointers. They formed an organization with strict rules. Hitler and Nazism had not yet come to prominence, but the principles of eugenics were stringently followed. All pups were inspected and tested at various stages of development. All pups that did not measure up to the high standards, no matter how cute and lovable, were killed. Once the gray breed was consistent, all lucky owners were ordered by the Weimaraner Committee when to breed their bitches, and with what stud dog.

Weimar is in mid-eastern Germany, south of Berlin. It was not until well after world War Two that the breed found its way to North America, and it was, indeed, a super race of canines.

Of course the strict standards could not be applied here – eugenics had become a dirty word thanks to Hitler. The breed declined and became just another hunting dog. Yet if one searched carefully, one could still find an intelligent, universal hunting Weimaraner.

All this Klaus Gipfel explained to Rick Amyotte as they sped in the morning mist by motor boat across Fourteen Island Lake to a wooded peninsula. Nobody much went there on foot as the base of the peninsula was mucky and reedy.

Five minutes after they had beached the craft in a small cove, Treu was on point, like a solid gray rock in the forest. Both hunters approached warily, for the Southern Ruffed Grouse, unlike its Northern cousin, is exceedingly skittish and wily.

With a thunder of wings, the bird flashed past Rick, quartering to his left and twisting into a space between two large hemlocks. In Rick's excitement, he pressed the trigger too soon and shot behind the fan tail. Klaus' 20 gauge spoke and the grouse tumbled.

Just as Rick was about to reload, another bird sprang out of an oak tree, streaking in the other direction. This one Rick dropped with his second barrel.

Treu made perfect retrieves on both birds. Somehow, Rick was not surprised.

Back at the mansion at noontime, as they were plucking and cleaning their game – five grouse, two woodcock and a mallard drake that had been feeding on aquatic arrowhead plants by the shore – Klaus got to the point.

"I don't often read the local newspaper, Rick. I'm more interested in business news and international affairs. But last night I went on the Internet, pulled up the Kingston Whig Standard and did a search for the name Amyotte. I didn't know about your daughter, Tanya. I'm very sorry to learn of your loss. I expect that is why you have come here, yet I still cannot see how I might help you."

Rick spoke slowly, in a neutral tone.

"In Tanya's purse, we found a match box with your son's initials and a telephone number. It belongs to a house on Cherry Street, in Kingston. Dieter is supposed to be in Belleville, still on parole, but he was there in Kingston last week, meeting with Alberto Golondrino, who had taken Tanya to New York. I'm trying to connect the dots."

Klaus nodded as he put the mallard's heart and liver in a plastic bag and rinsed off his hands and knife. He touched-up the blade on a small whetstone, wiped it with an oily rag, and sheathed it. "I wasn't going to tell you this. It will only add to your pain. But I recognized Tanya's picture in the newspaper. She used to buy some of her drugs from my son, Dieter."

Rick's shoulders sagged. "Drugs? Are you sure?"

Klaus straightened to his full height and looked into Rick's eyes. "You are a hunter, as I am. We're different from ninety-five percent of the population. We take responsibility for the death of the game, which nourishes us. We accept, even embrace the ugly, brutal side of nature, so that we can participate fully in it. Do you have the soul of a hunter, or do you want a Walt Disney myth?

"Give it to me straight, Klaus. Whatever you know, or even suspect. We both realize our kids are not angels."

"It was just before that dreadful night two years ago. I realized that Dieter was dealing drugs, and I went into Kingston to try to reason with him. That Czech cop, Sergeant Novak, had alerted me to some of Dieter's activities, and advised me to get him away from that crowd or he would likely get busted."

"Milos Novak? He was my ex-partner. He never said anything about this to me!"

"Maybe it was because he knew that Tanya was also involved. It wasn't hard stuff. Just a bit of pot, or hash oil, or a few amphetamines to get the kids through exam times. Tanya was a leader, Rick. If her fellow students wanted to do drugs, she'd supply them, and make a profit. Like Dieter, she was a mover and a shaker. And amphetamines, so my son claimed, actually calmed her down – like with Hyperactive Disorder kids."

"That explains a lot of what I didn't understand back then – her independence and defiance of me. It all made for marital chaos."

"Tell me about it. I've been there too, Rick. That day, when I went into Kingston, I argued bitterly with Dieter. I found his stash of drugs and flushed everything down the toilet. I told him he'd get no more money out of me for such sheep shit. It was then that he threatened to kill me. I left, because he was already out of control from drugs, and I was nearly there from rage."

"So when he arrived at night by snow-machine…"

"Stolen, by the way. But he did return it to the owner and got into his car, which he'd parked on the road, after you had left here."

"You called us because he renewed his threats?"

"Yes. It was two days after the ruckus in Kingston. But Dieter is able to fake-good. He's quite believable. When you showed up, he calmed down and was sweet as honey."

"Without the full picture, Klaus, I thought you two had had a little family spat, and it was over."

"So did I. I'm as responsible as you are for subsequent events."

"How about hard drugs – cocaine, heroin? Was Dieter dealing that?"

"Not so far as I could determine. That stuff is pretty well controlled by the biker gangs. He'd be stupid to cut into their turf. No, most of the cannabis he got from Alberto Golondrino. The rest was mainly prescription drugs, stolen from pharmacies or obtained by phony prescriptions. The pen is mightier than the sword, you know. That's why he went to the pharmacy in Sydenham that night. He was desperate for some Dilaudid. He didn't expect Miryam Tomari to be there, working so late. If he hadn't taken that damn gun... if...if... . You know the German saying?"

"Yeah. The dog and the rabbit. Life is full of ifs."

"You know, a strange thing happened while Dieter was in prison. He had a Case Management Officer who really took an interest in him, gave him every break he could, even helped him get early parole."

"It happens. Maybe this person saw some good in your son. Man or woman?"

"A man. But the curious thing is, this Case Management Officer is Abu Tomari. He's the son of Omar and Miryam Tomari. Miryam is the woman Dieter shot with my gun!"

* * *

CHAPTER EIGHT

Omar Tomari was troubled. The conference in Seattle had been potentially profitable because of the contacts he'd made. Meeting with international pharmacists and the representatives of pharmaceutical companies had given him a wider perspective, as did his contact with the herbal and alternative medicine crowd. It was the first time those people had been invited to such a gathering. Omar, with his background in Ayurvedic and Oriental Medicine, spoke their language and learned from them, which products had been clinically tested, and which ones were likely only placebo.

The trouble started with U.S. customs at Toronto's Pearson International Airport. Despite his Canadian passport, his birthplace (Uganda), his skin colour (brown, ethnic Indian) and his mustache, they treated him as though they thought he was Osama bin Laden in disguise. Canada Customs and Immigration scrupulously avoided ethnic profiling, but Team U.S.A. applied it routinely. The same thing happened on his flight home. Then he found that his Lexus, right next to the office at the Park and Fly, wouldn't start. The mechanic pointed out that someone had siphoned-off all the gas, as well as stealing his collection of CD's from the console.

Omar's main trouble, however, was familial, or more precisely, his wife, Miryam.

They had met when they were both studying pharmacy in England. Her people had come from Pakistan to the UK because they were out of favour with the current military junta that had assassinated the president of the day. His family came from Uganda because the excesses of the capricious Idi Amin made life too dangerous for Indian shopkeepers. Both Omar and Miryam were bright, healthy, attractive and Muslim. Their union was blessed by both families. Upon their graduation, they had come to Canada and set-up a pharmacy, for their training gave them Canadian licensure. Within ten years, they owned a string of pharmacies. They also had a son, Abu.

Abu. Omar didn't even like the name. It had been Miryam's choice. Abu Bakr had been Muhammad's father-in-law, and the first *Khalifa* or Deputy to guide the faithful after the Prophet's death. But Abu Sayef was the name of a Muslim fanatic in the Philippines, and the current name of the separatist, terrorist movement there. Omar might have forgotten this association if only Miryam had not insisted on sending Abu for six months to a *madrasa* in Pakistan, to be indoctrinated in the faith and in hatred of the West.

When Abu Tomari returned, he could recite the whole text of the *Qur'an*, and most of the deadly message, printed in an Arabic newspaper in London on 23 February 1998. It was "the Declaration of the World Islamic Front for Jihad against the Jews and the Crusaders." It was a historical, religious diatribe which concluded with a *fatwah*, or decree on religious law. Every Muslim who was able was "to obey God's command to kill the

Americans and plunder their possessions…and to launch attacks against the armies of the American devils and those who are allied with them from among the helpers of Satan." This was signed by leaders of the Jihad in Egypt, Pakistan and Bangladesh. One of the signatories was Osama bin Laden.

Miryam was always more devout than Omar. He sometimes forgot to pray five times a day, and even ate lunch occasionally during the holy month of Ramadan, to keep up his strength. Miryam kept the observances scrupulously, as did Abu after he returned from his indoctrination at the *madrasa*.

The west had been good to Miryam and Omar both, but she forgot all that when she got shot through the thigh by a ham-eating German. Then a drunken Catholic cop had put his unclean hands on her, without so much as asking her permission, or assuring that a male relative was present to safeguard her virtue.

Miryam's frantic telephone calls home for help went unheeded, largely because of what had happened just before.

The family had sat down to dinner together. Abu was home from Queen's University for the weekend. The discussion had turned to the Jihad; the armed struggle. Abu quoted some *hadiths* – traditions as to the interpretation of the Words of the Prophet. "Jihad is your duty. A day and a night of fighting on the frontier is better than a month of fasting and prayer. Paradise is in the shadow of swords."

Miryam decried the degeneracy of the West; rap music, public nudity, dirty dancing and homosexuality. She believed that Muslim men should be warriors and carry out God's will until the *Kefirs* (infidels) were expelled from Islam's holy places and Sharia law reigned supreme, as in the glory days of Islam in the Middle Ages.

Omar had grown angry. He, too, was a Muslim, but this command came, not from God, but from mad men. He, too, quoted some *hadiths* – "Be advised to treat prisoners well. God has forbidden the killing of women and children." The Prophet said, "Whosoever kills himself in any way will be tormented in that way in Hell."

"How can you say that this random terrorism, televised torture of hostages, suicide bombers maiming and killing thousands of innocents, is sanctioned by God? It's absurd!" Omar struck the table with his fist so hard that some cutlery and one plate fell on the floor.

Abu slyly implied his father was speaking as a Westernized coward. Miryam agreed. Omar was almost blind with rage, and went outside into the snow. (That was something he could never do as a youth in Uganda.)

To shelter himself from the wind, Omar went into the garden shed, next to the lawn mower and snow blower.

He heard an engine start in the garage. He peered out to see Miryam's vehicle emerge. Two heads were in it. She was taking Abu back to his residence in Kingston. Good. It gave them all time to cool off. Another family meal was ruined by the tentacles of Islamic Jihad.

Miryam didn't go directly home after driving Abu to his residence. She stopped off at their pharmacy in Sydenham on the way home. She thought some Zopiclone might help her settle down to sleep.

She had no idea that Dieter Gipfel had broken in, was desperately searching for Dilaudid, and was armed.

When Dieter saw a menacing figure, back lighted by the street lamps outside, he instinctively drew the Colt Trooper and fired. When he saw what he had done, he grabbed a box of Percocet, which would settle his withdrawal tremors, and fled out the back.

Sergeant Milos Novak arrested him that same snowy night on his way back to Kingston.

* * *

CHAPTER NINE

Karla MacTaggart drove her green Subaru Forester through the late October drizzle, which slicked the fallen leaves on the back roads from Tweed through Marlbank to Deseronto. She was a good driver and the vehicle sure-footed. Avoiding Highway 401, she drove by the edge of Tyendinaga Mohawk Territory and took Highway Two, and then the Loyalist Parkway all the way into Kingston.

The outdoors store in Tweed, re-named "Close to Nature" after her husband's death, sold mainly fishing and camping equipment, and guns. A pair of trusted employees would run it for the day.

Jim had died well before his three score and ten. Karla was left to raise her eighteen-year-old daughter, Noreen, on her own, and salvage what she could from the business. But she'd done it, single-handedly. She was resilient; always had been. But now, the death of her only grand-child, Tanya, gave an ache to her heart that almost suffocated her. How much longer could she keep on fighting, and for what?

As Karla drove by Millhaven and Bath Institutions; maximum and light medium security federal prisons, she unconsciously positioned her purse on the passenger seat a bit closer to her. One never knew what crafty crooks might be escaping at just that very moment.

The ferry had recently departed from the dock, taking passengers and vehicles over to Amherst Island, just west of Wolfe Island out in Lake Ontario.

Unlike the bold and impetuous James Wolfe, General Jeffrey Amherst had been a cautious and methodical plodder. At the very end of the 150 years of continual warfare between Britain and France, Amherst, with Wolfe's daring help, had captured the French Fort of Louisbourg in Nova Scotia, but then took two years to make his way through Lake Champlain for a planned attack on Montreal. By then, Wolfe had captured the citadel at Quebec, Montreal had fallen the next spring, and, apart from a final skirmish on Signal Hill in Newfoundland, it was all over. The French had lost their foothold in North America. Rule Britannia!

Karla still retained some French, from her childhood in Quebec, but she was glad the highway signs here were all in English. It made her feel she belonged here in Loyalist Ontario.

As she came by the Collins Bay United Church where the Memorial service for Tanya had been held, Karla's eye's welled-up again with tears. She pulled over to park at the boat launch and calm down. Although the rain was falling harder now – it always did in Kingston – Karla walked out on the dock to watch the skeins of low-flying cormorants winging toward the Brothers' Islands. Their toxic guano had killed most of the trees on those lovely little gems, and their voracious appetites had ruined the sport and commercial fisheries. Incredibly, the arm-chair naturalists had pressured the government to keep the cormorants on the protected list. As a flock of thirty swung by the dock, Karla wished fervently for a twelve gauge and a box of number four Hevi-shot. Given the chance, she'd be glad to do her bit to balance the eco-system!

By the time Karla had resumed her trip and found parking in the Underground Garage at Queen's University and Kingston General, her grief had turned to anger. She had deliberately taken the most southern route along King Street west, past the DuPont Company, which went by another name now, past the two jutting, angular-rectangular pieces of steel called the Time Sculpture, and past the bronze lion the kids climbed on at Richardson Beach, for she'd wanted to re-trace the route she'd run in last summer's Kingston Triathlon. She had taken first prize for women over sixty in the long course. That was easy, for she was the only woman over sixty. But she had also edged by the two women over fifty-five. Not bad for an old gal.

The rain lashed down like a monsoon as Karla ran the hundred metres from the Parking garage to Kingston General Hospital. She kept her purse clutched close to her breast, under her rain coat. At the Information Desk, she asked where to find Dr. Lucy Lam, in Toxicology.

She had to ask directions two more times in the labyrinthine corridors of Kingston General Hospital before she found her.

"How can I help you, Ms. MacTaggart?" Lucy asked.

"Please, call me Karla. I hadn't even met you until your Mom's funeral years ago, but I feel I know you. Evelyn and I kept in touch by mail after both our families left Quebec. And you showed up at Tanya's Memorial service, and did some further investigations. Whatever you can tell me that might help me understand more about her death would put my mind at ease. She was my only grand-child."

"Sometimes reality is ugly – the truth can be troubling." Lucy Lam looked away. "Have you spoken with Rick Amyotte about this?"

"No. We...we don't talk much. I try not to be judgmental and I recognize that blood is thicker than water as they say. But objectively, he was the cause of the divorce. With his whoring and drinking and domineering attitude to Tanya, Noreen had no choice but to kick him out of her life. But that's the past. Is he now poking around, doings some half-assed drunken investigation on his own? That fool would manage to fuck up the Lord's Prayer!"

Lucy got up, walked around the desk, and would have stared out the window, but there was none. She had to make do with a calendar with the picture of a sunrise behind Fort Henry, taken from the junction of the Cataraqui with the St. Lawrence River.

She turned to Karla. "It was Ketamine we found in Tanya's body. It is one of the three main date-rape drugs. The other two popular ones are GHB and Rohypnol. Ketamine is used as an anesthetic agent. It disinhibits; renders one unaware of what is going on, but the muscles are not paralyzed. It didn't kill Tanya – not in those concentrations. But it likely made her too confused to flee when the first plane hit the tower. Now whether she took the Ketamine voluntarily or even whether it was administered by mouth or by injection, we can't tell. Or it could have been an accident. Some people buy a drug, believing it to be one chemical, but it turns out to be another. That's all I know. Anything more would be pure speculation.

"Have you been talking with Rick about this?"

"Yes. I've tried to answer his questions." Lucy looked away again.

"So he is launching some kind of investigation – on his own, or with the help of Milos Novak?"

"Pretty much on his own, I believe."

"Oh, great! He'll muddy the waters so much we'll never get to the bottom of this…this presumed homicide." Karla frowned. "Where would one get Ketamine?"

"From a hospital. Or from a pharmacy that supplies hospitals."

"Like the Tomari Drug Warehouse? They no longer run a regular pharmacy, but stock drugs of all kinds. Would they supply Ketamine to the hospital pharmacy here?"

"I suppose so. They are the main supply source for all of South Eastern Ontario. But isn't your focus of interest a bit narrow?"

"You're right! Let's make a chart. May I?" Without waiting, Karla snatched up a note-pad, which had been lying face down on Lucy's desk. On it were written all the names that Karla was about to write:

Tanya Amyotte

Alberto Golondrino aka?

Omar Tomari	Dieter Gipfel
(Miryam Tomari)	Milos Novak
Abu Tomari	
Person(s) Unknown	

"This is exactly what Rick used to do when he was working on a case, but it's in your handwriting, Lucy."

"Yes. I wrote it down after talking with Rick. I thought it might be helpful."

"Why is Miryam's name bracketed?"

"You didn't hear?"

"Hear what?"

"Miryam and Omar separated last August. She rented a cottage on Crow Lake, near Sharbot Lake. Omar suspected she was suffering from a psychosis. She'd become more and more reclusive and began to dress in a full chador. A few days after 9-11, the day after the service for Tanya, in fact, her son Abu went to Crow Lake to see his mother. With him was Alberto Golondrino."

"I would have thought maybe Dieter Gipfel. I know he used to sell drugs to Tanya. Maybe some of them he got from the Tomari Pharmacy, or later, the Warehouse. But, Golondrino? He's an impresario. Is he into drugs?"

"Rick thinks perhaps. However, Alberto does have a line of cosmetics and health products through his Agency, and he might have been asking the Tomaris to make up some new product. Omar and Miryam are compounding pharmacists."

"I know," Karla replied. "My doctor still gets my bio-identical hormone creams from the Tomaris. Well, what next, Lucy?"

"Somehow, the visit must have been disturbing to Miryam. After Abu and Alberto left, Miryam went down to the township dump, dressed in her black chador. She walked right up to the black bears and began feeding them from a package of dates from Lebanon. The bears must have found them delicious. When the dates were gone, the bears pursued her, knocked her down, and clawed apart the chador, looking for more. She died from the mauling. Was it a suicide or an accident brought on by her psychosis? We'll never know. She didn't regain consciousness.

"I was in on the autopsy. Miryam was developing osteoporosis and had a Vitamin D deficiency. With no sunshine on her skin, she should have known enough to take supplemental D. Its deficiency can have an effect on the brain as well as the bones."

Karla shook his head. "That poor man!"

"Who?"

"Omar. I know him. I used to get my medications from one of his pharmacies. He's a very kind, gentle man."

"Well, let's not remove his name from the list just yet."

"Agreed. Like Inspector Clouseau, I suspect nobody, and I suspect everybody. What's the connection between Abu and Dieter Gipfel?" Karla asked.

"Because Abu Tomari speaks Arabic and is a Muslim, his rise in the Penitentiary Service was rapid. They need him to talk with the Islamic terrorists they have serving sentences, and the detainees they expect to have with the new Security Certificates. When he's not doing that, Abu is a Case Management Officer at Bath Institution. He was instrumental in obtaining Dieter Gipfel's parole. He seems to be pals with Milos Novak, who now is with the Pen squad."

"They might have met professionally. There's nothing to that," Karla observed.

"Maybe, but Rick thinks they are both wealthier than they deserve to be. Abu might be getting an extra allowance from his father. But Milos? Rick worked with him. He knows his circumstances. If he's suddenly rich, then it's likely something illegal, Rick says. With Dieter, and Alberto and Abu in the mix, it's probably drugs. And Tanya, your grand-daughter, was drugged when she died."

Karla's eyes narrowed, "I know Milos Novak too. He was a guest in my home back before Rick and Noreen separated. He comes across as a good guy, but he's a Czech. He lived under Communist rule until he escaped a year before the whole Communist Bloc imploded. The Czechs are a unique people. Surrounded by more powerful neighbours, mainly Germans and Austrians, often conquered and occupied, they have learned how to manipulate, dissimulate and work clandestinely. At first, I would have erased Milos' name. Now I'm not sure. Leave it for now."

"Let me make a photo-copy for you," Lucy said as she moved Karla's purse from the top of the copy machine. She lifted it thoughtfully. "What do you have in here, a gold brick from the Nordisque Mine?" Lucy joked.

"Gold is not the ultimate security. I have something better. I rarely leave home without it."

Lucy's Oriental eyes widened in surprise. "You're going about armed? In daylight, in the streets of Kingston, in a hospital? For the love of the Buddha, you're being a trifle paranoid, Karla. What if you get caught with this?"

"You haven't lived through what I have, Lucy. When Noreen was just eighteen, my husband, Jim Duncan, had a gun shop in Tweed. He had trained as a gunsmith. I helped him in the store. We stocked and sold firearms of all types – rifles, shotguns, even handguns, for, although they were restricted, all of our customers were law-abiding, target-shooting types.

"One evening, Jim was alone, just about to close, when three armed men broke in, tied him up, and began tossing all our guns into a van. Jim got free enough to reach a shotgun we kept under the counter. But, because of police pressures, we kept it unloaded and locked. Jim had just got the lock off and was reaching for a box of ammo when the thieves gunned him down."

Lucy knew there was no argument powerful enough to change Karla's stance. "Better to be judged by twelve than carried by six?"

"Yes! Exactly. And our Charter of Rights proclaims we have `the right to life, liberty and security of the person.´ I'm just claiming that right with my Browning Hi Power as a safeguard. I'm fully trained in firearms, and no law made by some bureaucrat is ever going to leave me disarmed and helpless like Jim was. And this applies especially when I'm embarking on an investigation into my grand-daughter's death!"

There was new respect in Lucy's eyes. She had studied Kung Fu, but a firearm in capable hands always trumped the most lightning high kick.

"Karla, why don't you and Noreen work directly with Rick on this? He has quit smoking, he's cut way back on his drinking, and he's working out with weights and on a bike. He plans to do the Kingston Triathlon next summer. Put your heads together, and you'll be a lot stronger."

"Or weaker. You've heard the expression, `None of us is as stupid as all of us together?´ Or, `A giraffe is a race horse designed by committee?´ It wouldn't work, Lucy. Noreen hates Rick. I don't, but I don't like him much, and he has promised to clean-up his act before, but always relapses."

"Well I don't intend to act as go-between with the feuding family," Lucy replied. "Be careful, Karla. I hope you never have to use that Browning."

"So do I. And thanks for your help." She picked up the photo copy Lucy had made, folded it, and put it in her gun-toting purse. She didn't need it, for she clearly understood the *dramatis personae.* She knew what her next move would be.

As she opened the door, Karla said, "Lucy, you be careful too. Rick Amyotte, he will break your heart."

* * *

CHAPTER TEN

O n the week-end before the first Monday in November, there is always a flurry of activity at the Frontenac Rifle and Pistol Club, for the firearms season for deer opens then. Sunday shooting is allowed at the range.

Rick Amyotte was at the handgun bunker. He had already filled his deer tag with a crossbow; behind his rural home, practically in his own back yard. He had enough venison for now. Instead of sighting in his rifle, Rick was blasting away at steel plates set up in the bunker with his Colt handgun, a Model 1911, .45 ACP.

He loaded the semi-automatic with eight fat, flat-pointed copper jacketed cartridges. The .45 relies on a wide, heavy but slow-moving slug. With this caliber, hollow points are not necessary for quick stops. The handgun is, after all, a short range, defensive weapon.

Adjusting his ear protection, Rick pushed the button on the timer, sitting on the table beside him, and waited for the beep.

It came in three seconds, shrill enough for him to hear through the muffs. Drawing with controlled speed, his finger outside the trigger guard, Rick raised the gun to meet the supporting hand, swept off the safety with his thumb, and pressed the trigger, eight times. Through the blue smoke, he could see he'd knocked down all five heavy plates and had two holes in the torso and one in the head of the paper target.

By habit, he removed the empty magazine, checked the chamber to see it was empty, lowered the slide, then the hammer and re-holstered.

Rick was just reaching to check the time when a voice behind him said, "Six point four-five seconds. That's good shooting, Rick." It was Karla MacTaggart, his former mother-in-law.

"Not bad, for me. It wouldn't win a match. Too slow, and one of those body hits is in the C-Zone.

"It would still shatter the arm of the bad guy – get his respect. Of course, that respect would all disappear with the head shot."

"I bet you'd do better with your nine-millimetre."

"No, I'd be a bit slower, but I'm accurate. You used to be too shaky to be a good handgun shot, Rick."

"Well, I got rid of all my tensions earlier with an eight K morning run today."

"My, my. Not smoking or drinking these days? How long is this phase going to last – until you earn your halo?"

"No, just for today," Rick replied, picking up on Karla's skepticism.

"Oh. One day at a time. I see. Do you go to AA meetings?"

"I used to, years ago. Now, I just apply the principles I learned, like staying sober one day at a time. Why are you here, Karla? Do you want to shoot a few rounds?"

"No. I shot with the Tweed Group on Thursday evening. I'm here to see if you have any binoculars, or a spotting scope, and would you lend them to me for a few minutes."

"Your leap in logic confounds me, Karla."

"Last week, I drove by Amherst and Wolfe Islands. After learning that the local legal Ketamine is supplied by the Tomari Pharmaceutical Warehouse, I decided to be resolute and act, like Wolfe, not putter about like Amherst. I went to confront Omar Tomari."

"And?"

"And I think he's a good guy. He's still grieving over his wife's death. But he's happy that his son, Abu, is over his youthful rebellion and is doing so well in the Penitentiary Service. Abu showed up while I was there. Everything seemed all right. He was cordial enough. But he's driving a big, black Lincoln Navigator. Those are pricey vehicles."

"Maybe his parents financed it."

"Omar says no. But Abu had gone to 'Next to Nature' in Tweed two weeks ago and purchased a Savage bolt action rifle in .243 Winchester calibre. He said he wanted it for target shooting, but he bought ten boxes of 100 grain soft point ammo."

"And target shooters use full metal jacket. The .243 is good for varmints with the 75 grain hollow-points. The 100 grain is usually used for deer. It's a bit light for bear or moose."

"But deadly on humans. And flat-shooting, accurate," Karla observed.

"Yeah, it would be. Zero it at two hundred metres. It will only be about three centimeters high at one hundred and ten centimeters low at three hundred. That's the width of your hand, fingers together. I certified Abu as being firearm-safe in a course I taught last year. I hope I didn't make a mistake. But he's legally entitled to his rifle, Karla."

"I know. But he didn't want a scope. You and I know one can be ten times more accurate with a good scope."

"Perhaps he has another source for a scope."

"He has. I followed Abu here. I'm doing a bit of private surveillance. He's over there on the rifle range with another guy who arrived in a maroon Dodge Durango. They appear to be attaching a scope. When I saw your vehicle, I came over here. I don't want to blow my cover, or whatever it is you law-enforcement types say. Now do you have binoculars or a scope?'

"The latter. In the truck. I'll get it."

It was a pricey "Himalaya" spotting scope, made by Summit Industries and given to Rick by Klaus Gipfel himself after one of their hunting out-ings together. He set it up on a dirt berm on its tripod, and slid a folding, three-legged stool behind it.

"The plot thickens," Rick muttered as he focused on the two men at the far end of the rifle range. "Have a look."

Karla sat down and peered through the crystal-clear optics. "There's Abu. The rifle does have a scope mounted now. Who is that other man, wearing blue and white urban camo?"

"That's Abu's former client in the Joint, Dieter Gipfel. It looks to me like the scope is a Gold Peak, also made by Summit."

Karla was still peering through the powerful optics. "Dieter is about to shoot now, probably at the two-hundred metre butt."

"He'd better not! There are three other people checking their targets at their end of the one hundred. The flag is up. He won't shoot. He'd be sending slugs right by them."

Dieter did – three rounds cracking out in quick succession.

"Stay here," Rick ordered. He strode over to the rifle range, his .45 weighing ominously on his right hip.

"You," he barked like a drill Sergeant, jabbing a finger at Abu, "are a member here. I've taught you safe gun handling. You should know better than to give a rifle to this worthless ignorant chunk of porcupine shit. He's prohibited from laying hands on a firearm for five years!"

Dieter spoke. The rifle was still in his hands, and the barrel swung toward Rick. "Well, it's Dudley Do-Right, super cop, or ex-cop. Those people weren't in any danger. But you are, accosting me, armed and belligerent, obviously trying to get revenge for losing your job – through your own incompetence."

They were all frozen in space, except for the rifle-barred which was creeping by millimetres toward Rick's chest.

"Dieter," Abu pleaded, "Put the rifle down. There is no need to make a bad situation worse."

"Especially since my nine-millimetre is pointed at your crotch," Karla said, for she'd slipped in behind the men and over to one side.

Dieter shrugged and placed the rifle on the sandbags. "See it was unloaded," he said as he opened the bolt. A spent cartridge case flipped out. There was another live round nestled in the magazine.

"Dieter," Rick said quietly, "Your pal here, Abu Tomari is a Peace Officer. He could arrest you. He obviously won't, because he's been unwise enough to loan his firearm to you, a person he knows is under prohibition. And I won't proceed officially by calling my cop-friends because your father believes you are on the verge of straightening-out. I hope he's not wrong. But if I ever see you again with a gun in your hands, I'm going to ram the barrel so far up your ass that the front sight will scratch your palate. Now get your sorry self out of here!"

Then, as if for emphasis, the rain beat down like hail on the narrow tin roof of the firing line. They all scurried for cover.

Dieter left first, gunning his Durango with the SCOOTER license plates so hard that the gravel flew like bullets.

Karla noticed that Abu's shoulders were shaking as he cased his new rifle. Whether it was from fright, or hysterical laughter or from sobs, she could not tell.

If Rick noticed this, he didn't let on.

And down at the two hundred metre butt, the dripping target had three holes in the black that one could cover with a toonie. Dieter Gipfel might be a scofflaw, but he sure could shoot.

* * *

CHAPTER ELEVEN

The statue of Sir John A. Macdonald, Father of Confederation, had an icicle hanging from his prominent nose. It was typical Kingston weather for early February – frigid, damp and nasty. A few mallards hung about on West Street at the boat ramp down to Lake Ontario. People fed them bread crumbs or grain, delaying any southward migration. In a sudden cold snap, they'd freeze into the harbour, and those same people would say it was too bad, Nature can be cruel, not realizing that their interference in the natural order of things was causing the death of ducks.

West Street, which is in the Eastern part of modern Kingston, merges with Lower Union, which runs past the park where the impassive statue stands, by the court house and on to Earl.

Around Earl and Lower Union, there are elegant old limestone houses, mixed with more modest abodes. One of these housed the Wong Travel Agency.

Elizabeth Wong, known as Betsy, was on the telephone, speaking in Mandarin. "You'd better get over here," she said to her friend, Dr. Lucy Lam. "You asked me to watch for certain names. Three guys are here right now, and I think you might be interested."

The Wong Travel Agency was not far from Kingston General Hospital. Lucy was there in fifteen minutes.

Canadians get restless in the depth of winter. They long for a break – somewhere warm and sunny. Lucy looked through some pamphlets which offered sun, sand, palm trees, romance, adventure – enough to satisfy any true sybarite – while the three men made their arrangements.

After the trio left, Lucy had her friend reserve two seats on a flight to Cancún, Mexico.

* * *

"I can't go, Rick," Lucy said to him. "I've been subpoenaed as an expert witness in an important trial. I can't leave Kingston now. Karla can't go either. She has a booth rented at the Outdoor Show in Toronto. That leaves Noreen." They were talking in Lucy's basement office in KGH.

"I'd rather die," Rick growled. "Besides, your scheme to get us to work together on this included Karla, but not Noreen. Does she know everything that we do?"

"Probably. I told Karla. She would tell Noreen. After all, she was Tanya's mother. And Noreen is involved with volunteer work for impoverished women in the Third World. It would be a perfect cover for her to go with you. Both your passports have the name, Amyotte. Your divorce isn't final."

"Are you trying to reconcile us, Lucy? Because it is not going to happen."

Lucy looked at him thoughtfully. "I'm not much of an adventuress, Rick. I'd rather test-out you and Noreen together again, than fall for you, only to have my heart broken. So far, we have made no promises to each other, and I won't commit myself until all this shakes out."

"Is Noreen willing to go to Mexico, with me?"

"Karla says yes; she'll go reluctantly. Go to Cancún with her, Rick. Betsy Wong can get you there direct from Ottawa. You would arrive one day before the other three, who are leaving from Toronto. She has a reservation for you in the same resort in Playa del Carmen on the Mayan Riviera. You'll be able to scout-out the place before Abu Tomari and Dieter Gipfel arrive there."

"And what about Alberto Golondrino? Where is he staying?"

"Not there. From Cancún he's catching a connecting flight to Georgetown, Guyana. He's scheduled to return to Canada on the same flight as Abu and Dieter, but how he's getting back to Mexico remains a mystery. Maybe a private jet. He has the money for it."

Rick shook his head. "I'm trying to connect the dots, but coming up empty. Why on earth would Golondrino go to Guyana? That's way down in South America, the other side of Venezuela. What's there for him?"

"Maybe some tropical herbs for his beauty business. I hear he's interested in Maca, the sexual stimulant, but that is grown mainly in Peru, not Guyana."

"Do you have Internet access?" Rick gestured to Lucy's computer.

"Of course, I use it a lot for scientific references."

"Google Guyana for me. Let's see what we can find out."

A half hour later, they were not much wiser. Guyana is a former British Colony, is very poor, mainly exports aluminum and bauxite. Unlike its wealthier neighbour, Surinam, which was given to the Dutch by Britain in exchange for New Amsterdam, now New York City, it barely struggles along. English is the predominant language. Ex-slaves from Africa and East Indian shopkeepers made up a large part of the country and their descendant still dwell there.

"Just a moment," Lucy said. She picked up the telephone and spoke quickly in Mandarin.

"We may have something," she told Rick after hanging up. "Both Guyana and Surinam have substantial Muslim populations. In fact, they are the only two nations which are in the Western Hemisphere and have membership in the OIC, the Organization of the Islamic Conference. The rest are mainly in Africa and the Middle East. But what is more interesting is that Alberto Golondrino is using his Canadian passport to fly. It's under his original name, Iqbal Ghali Ruiz, birthplace, Mexico City. The Ruíz would be his mother's maiden name."

"Iqbal Ghali? A Mexican Muslim? I would have bet drugs, but does this or does it not hook into Islamic terrorism? The attack on the Twin Towers certainly was, and he was there. Abu Tomari has been brain-washed in a madrasa. But I can't quite see the connection."

"That is why you are going to Mexico with Noreen – to find out. Good luck, and happy holidays." Lucy got up from behind her desk and kissed Rick. She hung on longer and tighter than in a simple, friendly farewell.

"There is one other thing I forgot to mention," she said as Rick was opening the door. "After I left the travel agency, I saw Abu Tomari sitting in an unmarked car parked on Earl Street, passenger side. The engine was idling, polluting the atmosphere unnecessarily. I was annoyed enough to glare at the driver. It was your ex-partner, Milos Novak."

* * *

CHAPTER TWELVE

Rick Amyotte and his estranged wife, Noreen did not speak much on the flight from Ottawa to Cancún. The charter plane left at an ungodly time in the morning, the seats were too squished together for Rick's long legs to be comfortable, and the in-flight movie was a chick-flick – a lot of dialogue and not much action. Noreen watched it. Rick tried to snooze.

She was pleased to see that he ordered orange juice instead of booze when the flight attendants came by with drinks.

It was not until they descended through the cloud cover and could see the ocean, shallow and turquoise, inside the long coral reef, and the impenetrable jungle, thick, low and thorny, clothing the land down to the white sand beaches, that they began communicating something other than their leaden aloofness.

"Rick, did you ask Milos to run a CPIK on Alberto Golondrino, aka Iqbal Ghali?"

"I did. He said there was nothing."

CPIK is the police record of arrests and disposition of every criminal in Canada; a national rap-sheet.

"That surprises me. I thought he might be implicated in something."

"It surprised me too. Especially since I only mentioned the name Golondrino, not Ghali, and he didn't even tell me the guy has an alias. So I asked another cop-friend to run a CPIK under Golondrino too. It came up, large as life. So did his Mexican-Arab name, arrested on a drug and a firearm charge years ago, acquitted on both. That's how he got to be a Canadian citizen. He sold out his accomplices to get a walk and a friendly citizenship judge."

"Now why would Milos withhold that information from you, Rick?"

"I'd be guessing, and yours would be as good as mine. We'll have to wait and see."

The plane touched down with a slight lurch, then slowed smoothly as it made its way toward the waiting buses. The passengers applauded, realizing that ninety percent of aircraft fatalities occur when it hits the ground, and they had cheated death again.

Rick was just glad to stretch his legs.

* * *

As they queued up for Customs and Immigration, a hawk-nosed Arab in a long white robe, a string of black pearl "worry beads", red and white *keffiyeh* head cloth strode past them to a privileged desk, closed to the *hoi poloi*. His sun glasses failed to conceal the scar, which ran down his cheek from his left eye.

"He probably got that scar from a falconry accident," Rick muttered. He turned and looked out the wide window. "Look at the bird he rode in on."

It was a private, twin-engine Beechcraft jet, with the same checkering on the tail as on the Arab's *keffiyeh*.

The Arab was not so fortunate in getting his luggage passed. The problem seemed to be an aluminum case. He was arguing with the Customs officer in halting but grammatical Spanish as Noreen and Rick were lining up to push the lucky button. A red signal meant there would be inspection of their baggage, a green meant not. Apparently Mr. Mahmoud Khalid had been unlucky, and pushed red. That was the name the dark, Mayan, round-faced Customs officer called him as they dickered.

Digging in a tooled goatskin gentleman's handbag, Khalid extracted some keys to unlock the case, and produce some documents. With the documents were several thousand-peso notes.

The Arab continued his explanation as the official opened the case.

Rick could see a rifle with a Gold Peak Summit Industry scope mounted.

The officer compared the notation on the document with the data stamp on the barrel. *"Dos ciento, cuarenta y tres,"* he said, and handed back the document without the money. Smiling broadly, he said *"Todo está en ordén. Que tenga una buena estancia."*

As they walked out to the taxi stands, dodging the "sharks" who were trying to trap them into a time-share promotion, Rick asked, "Did he say that rifle was a .243? You studied Spanish in University, Noreen. What did Hawkeye say?"

"Hawkeye's name is Mahmoud Khalid. He's from Guyana. He's here to visit a ranch and do some hunting. And the rifle is a .243. Why, does that mean anything?"

"Probably not," Rick growled. "But it happens to be the exact same make of rifle and scope that Dieter Gipfel and Abu Tomari were shooting at the Club last fall."

As they left the airport in a taxi, they could see Señor Khalid getting into a Range Rover with his aluminum case. They could also see Hawkeye's plane taking off again, heading for who knows where.

* * *

Playa del Carmen sits sixty kilometres south of Cancún. Its beaches are sheltered, not only by the barrier reef, but by the Island of Cozumel, just four kilometres off its shore. Twenty years ago, it was just a quaint fishing village. Now it is totally geared to the tourist industry and has a population of 250,000.

Their resort was of white-washed domed Moorish design, unlike all the others, which mainly had the more rectangular-pyramidal Mayan architecture. It was a gated, secure resort hotel on one of the best stretches of beach. To the two Canadians fleeing the frozen north, The Hotel Loro del Moro, The Moor's Parrot, was as close to paradise as they could imagine.

"How are we going to pay for this?" Rick gestured to the three consecutive swimming pools, each two hundred metres long and forty wide, each with swim-up bars where one simply signed for drinks. The bill came at the end.

"So long as I contact the local office of the Women's Aid Organization I work for, my hotel expenses are paid. Mom paid for my air fare."

"Karla did that? I have no such fairy godmother. Lucky you."

"On a holiday, there is one major rule. No bitching," Noreen said. "I'll forego your alimony payments for the next two months, if you promise not to bitch. We'll split the hotel bill down the middle and I'll pay half. Agreed?"

"How could I refuse?" Rick said.

* * *

Pablo Fierro was a bright young man. He had only come to Quintana Roo from the neighbouring State of Campeche two years ago, and already he could speak some English and was assistant to the Concierge at the Loro del Moro. It was the business of the Concierge to smooth out the difficult details and formalities – *los trámites* – for the wealthy guests. Pablo was well-positioned to know the comings and goings of every one of them, so long as he kept his eyes and ears open.

He knocked on the door of the gringo couple from Canada. He wondered why this couple would need a two-bedroom suite. It was big enough to house Pablo's parents and all eight of his siblings too.

Noreen opened the door. Pablo was glad it was she, for he now could converse in Spanish. She understood Spanish, but he had to speak slowly and clearly for her to comprehend; as she'd explained when she'd hired him.

"The men in whom you have an interest, they have arrived. They are in the next building, room 3322."

She nodded, slipped him a hundred-peso note and asked, "Anything else?"

Pablo shifted in the doorway, uncomfortably, and lowered his head. "*Sí*," he said.

"Come in, please," Noreen said.

Once he was inside and the door closed, he explained, "They have a taxi ordered for tonight at ten-thirty. They are going to a…a… Gentlemen's Club. It's called `Con Macho Gusto,´ this club."

"Good. Why are you being so secretive Pablo? The name is just a play on words; close to `Con Mucho Gusto´ – `With great Willingness or Appreciation´. Is this club popular here in Playa del Carmen?

Pablo nodded. "With some types, yes, it's popular."

"What types?" Noreen persisted.

"*Maricones*. The ones who like teen-age boys. It's a Gay Club."

* * *

When Rick returned to the Loro del Moro Hotel, dawn was streaking the sky behind the palm trees, which stood between the swimming pools and the ocean. Noreen could tell he'd been drinking; not drunk, but definitely a bit glassy-eyed.

"How was the Con Macho Gusto Club?" she asked, trying to keep the anger out of her tone.

"A gay place to spend an evening. And yes, I did have a few drinks. I had to fit in. I don't know the Spanish for orange juice, and I do know the word for Margarita. Amazingly, it's Margarita. Works every time." He smirked.

"Tell me every last detail," she demanded. "Did you meet any cute guys there? Possible soul-mates?"

"There were a lot of cute guys. They were all supposedly over seventeen, but I'll bet at least half were no older than fourteen. The Club still had decorations up from Valentine's Day last week, and a couple of boys came on stage dressed as Cupids and sang love songs.

"I noticed a few foxy babes there too, and got into a conversation with one. She was from Cincinnati, with the emphasis on the Sin, she said. Turned-out she was a fag in drag. Almost had me fooled."

"You got to know her – or him – well-enough to tell for sure?"

"For sure. Yeah."

"That must have been fun. A gay old time. Stop rambling, Rick. Did you find out anything useful amidst your lewd encounters?"

"Abu and Dieter enjoyed the show, but seemed to be waiting for someone. That someone came into the Club around midnight. It was our Arab friend, Hawkeye, this time dressed like a rich, gay Mexican."

"Mahmoud Khalid? And he met with Dieter Gipfel and Abu Tomari?"

"He did. He danced with each of them. Obviously, he can't come out of the closet in his own Muslim society in Guyana. Here in sybaritic Playa del Carmen, he can show his true colours – rainbow, I think."

"Your homophobia is showing, Rick. Anything else?"

"Yeah. In the parking lot out back, just before they retired for the night, I don't know where, Khalid gave them a big fat briefcase and that aluminum gun case. We know what is in the gun case. I'm going to try to find out what is in the briefcase. See if Pablo Fierro can get a pass key from the Concierge. I'll search their room when they are out of it. But first, I'm going to get some shut-eye." He turned toward his bedroom.

"When you wake-up, Rick, I hope you have enough of a hangover to convince yourself to stay sober for the next twenty-four hours."

"That's the way it usually works. I was tempted to pick up a bottle of tequila on the way back but fought off the urge. Besides, the liquor stores were all closed."

"How noble of you, Rick. Praise God for small mercies." Noreen slammed the door to her bedroom.

* * *

CHAPTER THIRTEEN

The street that runs parallel to the beach, one block up in Playa del Carmen spouts forth a cacophony of sights, smells and sounds at night. It is blocked to vehicular traffic. People stroll up and down, making purchases of sandals, beachwear, cigars, booze, luggage, jewelry or sampling the fare of the numerous restaurants. Mariachi bands roam around, playing for a hundred pesos a song. Plaques put up by the city every fifty metres or so tell the story, in Spanish and English, of each of the hundred or so ancient Mayan gods with unpronounceable names and bloody, magical powers.

Rick and Noreen were tailing three men walking together fifty metres or so ahead of them. The gay Arab, Mahmoud Khalid, continued on down to the road, which led to the Marina. Abu Tomari and Dieter Gipfel turned into a restaurant, "The Merry Mariachi."

"You hang out here and see if those two order dinner," Rick suggested. "I'll keep an eye on Hawkeye. If it looks like they're going to be in there a while, meet me at the entrance to the Marina in fifteen minutes. If not, stay with them and I'll meet you in an hour at the Casa de Tequila."

"Who elected you Boss?" Noreen asked. "Yes, all right, I'll do it."

At the darkened Marina, Rick momentarily lost sight of the Arab, than saw him climbing aboard a private yacht.

By the lights on the pier, he could make out the name of the craft: "La Cime du Plaisir", out of Montreal.

Fifteen minutes later, the Arab was still negotiating with the vessel's Captain as Noreen arrived at the arched entrance to the Marina, rather breathless.

"They're settling in for drinks and dinner. Rick, this would be a good time to search their room! I obtained the pass key for only a few hours. Pablo Fierro says if anything goes missing, he's calling the cops on us. Get in and out quickly and learn what you can. Room 3322. Our flight out of here is the day after tomorrow. The others don't leave until Sunday."

"I know, and I don't work well under pressure. You're wearing those light sandals. I can move faster. Give me the key and I'll be back in our suite in a half-hour."

As Rick hurried past the restaurant, he had his head down. This did not prevent Dieter from recognizing him. It is difficult to be absolutely invisible in surveillance.

* * *

As Rick suspected, the briefcase was too big to fit into the security safe in room 3322. He found it behind Dieter's suitcase in the closet.

As he opened it on the king-size bed as big as a Ping-Pong table, two bubble-wrapped, multiple dose vials labeled Ketamine tumbled out, together with some syringes and needles. A printed sheet gave average anesthetic doses in milligrams per kilogram for intravenous or intra-muscular injection. A penned addendum at the bottom indicated the number of millilitres of that solution, given orally, to render the average date unable to resist a rapist. "Ha-ha!" was scratched in after this information.

The main bulk of paper-work was partly in English, but mainly in Arabic script. It seemed to contain detailed plans for building bombs and detonators out of commonly-available hardware, household items and chemicals.

In the bottom of the briefcase, a small zip-lock plastic envelope had a paper-wrapped packet inside. Rick hesitated, and then decided they wouldn't likely dust it for fingerprints. Smooth plastic holds prints far better than paper or leather.

The envelope contained twelve realistic-looking Quebec birth-certificates, probably forged. Each bore a different name; all of them Muslim males. The birth dates would put them all between twenty and forty years old.

He tried to sear the names into his memory, but it was no use. He was over his allotted time. Quickly placing everything back in order, he plunked the briefcase back behind the luggage as he'd found it.

On the way out, he saw a travel voucher on the office table for a trip to the Mayan ruins at Tulum. The date was tomorrow's.

Safely back in his own suite, he gave the pass key back to Noreen.

"I'll go stash this where Pablo told me to. He's on duty until midnight. You're sure your visit will go undetected?"

"Pretty sure. I had to hurry. By the way, we're going to Tulum tomorrow."

"It's about time we soaked up some history and culture. Here, anybody can get a sun-tan," Noreen said as she left.

Rick had not noticed a very fine piece of monofilament fishing line, half the length of his thumb that had been inserted under the buckle of that brief-case. It now lay on the floor of the closet in Room 3322.

* * *

CHAPTER FOURTEEN

Tulum was built in the late classical period of the Mayan Empire, over eight hundred years ago. Unlike the other ancient Mayan sites like Chichen Itzá, it was situated on the sea-coast, for it was a centre for trade.

The Mayans were brilliant astronomers and mathematicians. They were prone to line up buildings and windows to coincide with the rising of the sun on the solstices and the equinoxes, and with the rising and setting of the planet Venus, of which they were inordinately fond. They understood the concept of zero even before the Arab scholars. Their language, though it looks hieroglyphic, is actually phonetic. Tourists can get their initials, engraved in silver or gold in the Mayan alphabet, on an amulet which is "guaranteed to bring good luck", for only a few hundred bucks

"The down side was," as the guide explained to the group, "the soil here is very thin. As they cleared the surrounding jungle, they could grow crops for only a few years. And the gods dictated the times for planting, harvesting and for war. The gods demanded human sacrifices to assure good fortune in these ventures. Warfare, and the capture of prisoners to be sacrificed to the gods, was a religious duty, which the Mayans practiced devoutly. That and disease too, wiped-out their great civilization. By the time the Spanish conquistadores arrived, these buildings were well on their way to being ruined.

"See what a great comfort religion is to mankind?" Rick whispered to Noreen.

"Not all religions are equal," she replied. "Look, Abu and Dieter seem to be leaving their group, heading down to the south end of the beach. I guess we should follow."

"Suits me," Rick said. "The guide said it was a nude beach for those so inclined. Maybe I can catch a little titillation while we practice our surveillance."

"Please try to contain yourself, Rick."

Most of the bathers in the turquoise waters inside the barrier reef wore swim suits. A few women were topless. The only two men who went completely nude were gay and soon walked arm in arm to the shade behind a huge boulder.

Rick and Noreen followed Dieter to where the path on the cliff above the beach ended at the south rampart. There was a stone look-out post there. They got in it for some shade, for the sun's rays drove down on their heads and backs like molten iron.

"We're Canadian, and it is winter, eh? We can't complain about the heat here. Do you see Abu?" Rick asked.

"No. Dieter is taking up position on that flat rock over there." She was looking through the zoom lens of her camera. "He has the aluminum gun case."

"He'll cook like a baked iguana out there unless he has a lot of sunscreen on. Get a picture, Noreen, just for the record."

Below them, a security guard with his plastic I.D. fluttering around his neck was making his way to the beach below with great effort. It was a deserted cove, as no true paths led there, and towering rocks barred access from either side.

"Focus on that guy down there," Rick commanded. "What is he doing?"

"Probably just patrolling. Wait! It's Abu. With his brown complexion, he looks like a Mayan. He's disguised himself as a security guard!"

"Different kind of Indian, is our Abu. Something's about to go down."

What went down a few minutes later was a large bale, dropped into the sea by the Arab's Beechcraft with the checkered pattern on the tail. It bobbed there on the waves, while the plane headed north-east toward the Island of Cozumel.

"What now?" Noreen asked.

"We wait. It's what surveillance is all about. Ninety-five percent boredom; only five percent action."

A half-hour later, a shallow-draft speed boat buzzed over the horizon to the bale. With considerable difficulty, the two men on board were able to lift the package onto the open deck. Then the craft headed straight into the cove, negotiating expertly through a small break in the barrier reef.

"Well, well. Guess who is coming to dinner!" Rick exclaimed.

"I see. He's like a bad penny. He always turns up," Noreen said.

It was Alberto Golondrino. He and the boatman rode a wave in to shore and rolled the bale up onto the sand.

Then an argument ensued. Rick guessed it was over money. Although the two men were yelling at each other, their words were indistinct in the trade wind blowing from the vast Atlantic.

In a decisive gesture, the boatman strode back to his craft, possibly to get a weapon to settle the dispute.

Like an over-ripe melon, his brown head exploded in a shower of bone, brain and eyeball, as Dieter's rifle rang-out from the overlooking rock.

Abu joined Golondrino in the cove. With the help of the next large wave, they pushed the boat, with the corpse, out to sea, where it rocked gently and gradually further southward. Carrion birds were already circling around the floating dinner dish.

"Rick, shouldn't we do something?" Noreen asked.

"If we make a move, we're dead," he replied. "Put a fresh battery in that camera. Those guys down there aren't going to sit and guard that bale all night."

Once the evidence of the murder had floated away, Dieter Gipfel, the rifle back in its box, made his way down the same steep slope as Abu had.

An hour before the sun set behind them, Rick and Noreen saw Le Cime du Plaisir anchor just outside the reef. A large Zodiac inflatable motored through the reef to the cove. At the helm was Hawkeye-- Mahmoud Khalid – dressed once again as an Arab.

With the bale on board, there was barely enough room for the three men. They made it back to the Canadian yacht, which turned north toward Playa del Carmen.

"You get all of that on film?" Rick asked.

"No. It's a digital camera. But I got it all."

"No film? My, what will they think of next!"

"What's your take on all this, Rick?"

"The bale is probably South American cocaine. It will be used to finance the infiltration of a dozen al-Qaida terrorists into Canada. They are planning to blow up something, for the greater glory of Allah. That yacht should be going up the St. Lawrence to Montreal by the end of March. There are plenty of places where they can drop off the coke along the way, and plenty of places in rural Quebec to train a bunch of Islamist fanatics. Where the target is, and when it will be is as yet unknown. But that slime ball there is the same one who killed our daughter!"

"Alberto Golondrino? Yes, I'm sure of it too. And you won't rest until you take him out, legally or otherwise, Rick?"

"Legally or otherwise."

"What's that about the yacht? 'The Peak of Pleasure'?"

"Or `the Summit of Pleasure.´ I telephoned Lucy last night, asked her to check the registration of that boat. She said that Karla would be the best one to do so, since she deals in boats and other outdoor gear. She telephoned this morning while you were out swimming."

"Mom did? What did she say?"

"The boat, Le Cime du Plaisir, is owned by Klaus Gipfel, CEO of Summit Industries."

* * *

The bulk of the other tourists had left Tulum on their buses. Rick and Noreen were amongst the last stragglers to go through the gate.

As they walked the few hundred metres back to the parking area, a police officer and a security guard approached them. The policeman showed his badge. "*Señor* Amyotte y *Señora* ?" he asked. He showed them a gold-toothed smile.

"*Sí. Los mismos*," Noreen answered.

"Will you come with us please? We have a few questions for you. Then we take you right back to your hotel – the Loro del Moro, correct?

"I guess so." Rick had an uneasy feeling when he saw the unmarked vehicle.

The policeman got in the back seat with Rick. His belly bulged over his cartridge belt and the .38 Special rounds in the loops. The revolver was a Brazilian Taurus, a cheap clone of the Smith and Wesson. The safety strap was unhooked and folded back.

Noreen sat in the front with the Security guard, who was the driver.

"*Muy caliente* today," the policeman observed. "You get very hot out there in the sun. I suggest we stop for a drink. Then we can conclude our investigation in more comfort. *De acuerdo?*"

Rick nodded. "I could use a drink about now," he said. "A nice, cold Margarita, on the rocks, not blended."

"You like Margaritas? I take you to a place make the best Margaritas in all Quintana Roo!"

* * *

CHAPTER FIFTEEN

Since the State election, Augusto Guzman's fortunes had taken a down-turn. No, for a while, it was more like a free-fall. He had worked hard to become a policeman – got to know the right people; bribed the Captain who hired him. When the PRI formed the government, things were corrupt, but well-ordered. Everyone knew how the game was played, and one could make a comfortable living while still maintaining some semblance of law and order.

Then the PAN came to power. *Carajo*! Things all changed. Every PRI supporter lost employment. They were replaced by PAN henchmen. Of course the corruption continued; this, after all is Mexico, but Augusto found himself outside the loop.

Augusto still had his gun, which he'd had to buy himself, and his uniform. He also had his sly intelligence. It was much more difficult to shake down the bars and brothels for protection money, but still possible. That, and a bit of drug-dealing kept him supplied with whores, tequila and *la hierba*, a traditional Mexican weed the gringos call "Mary-Jane."

In recent months, however, the new Captain of the *Policía* Detachment had become annoyed with ex-constable Augusto Guzmán. It was just because he'd slapped around a madame in a prestigious whore-house for not paying him enough protection money. This madame was a favourite with the new Captain, and he was angry when he saw her beautiful nose, all mashed and broken. He had begun leaning heavily on Augusto, and the latter's sources of *dinero* were getting as dry as the *arroyo* in April.

That is why Augusto had readily accepted the commission from the rich Arab to take care of a little problem he had, or more precisely, two problems.

Oscar, his driver, was sober for now. He would be no impediment. A bottle of rum and a hundred pesos would satisfy him for making a simple drive into the country.

The red-head had freckles. She used a lot of sun screen, obviously, for she was but lightly tanned. She sat in the front seat, beside Oscar. Augusto couldn't see the startling blue eyes he'd noticed before, nor the full breasts like juicy half-grapefruits. He'd get to them later. Maybe.

The gringo beside him in the back seat might be a problem. He was darker, medium tall, but not gangly – the type who pumps iron. That is why the Moor had given Augusto that little flask of medicine – just some lubrication to make his task easier.

La Cántara Llena sat on the outskirts of town, almost at the edge of the thorny jungle. It meant "The Full Jug", just like the red-head's breasts. The cantina had been closed for the last week for some renovations. Augusto had paid the *cantinero* to open tonight for a few hours for this private gathering. The official opening would not be until tomorrow.

The sun had already set behind the mountains when Oscar parked in the lot behind *La Cántara Llena*.

"Come in, *amigos*," Augusto said, revealing his gold tooth in a broad smile. "We'll have a nice cold drink and conduct our business in a little Mexican minute."

The *cantinero* was behind the bar when they entered.

"I'll be your waiter, tonight," said Augusto. He went to the bar and got a Margarita for Rick, a Piña Colada for Noreen, and a Coke for himself. It was easy slipping the clear medicine into their drinks; a lot for the guy, a little for the red-head, for he had a plan forming in his mind.

"I don't drink alcohol while on duty," he explained piously between gulps of Coke from the bottle. He glimpsed Oscar eying the Bacardi bottle behind the bar. "Give the driver one drink of his choice," he told the bar-man. "Then you can go. I'll lock up."

Noreen looked alarmed, for she understood the Spanish. She noticed that Rick had downed almost all his Margarita in a couple of swigs. How could he do that, and not get a brain-freeze?

"Now, my friends, please tell me whether you saw anything unusual there at Tulum," Augusto asked.

"The architecture, the temples, the astronomical lay-out were all unusual," Noreen said as she sipped on her Piña Colada, and smiled back at him.

"I mean something *los turistas* might not see regularly."

"A boat came into the cove," Rick admitted. "I don't know how it got through the reef. I remarked on that to Noreen. Then we left and went looking for the sacred ball-court. Officer, I have to use the *baños*. Where are they?"

"Oscar will show you," Augusto said. He didn't want Rick taking off on him and causing any trouble. That was why he paid Oscar to be there.

"Did you take pictures there with your digital camera?" Augusto asked, gesturing to the camera still slung over her shoulder.

"Yes, of course." Noreen had another sip. The drink tasted slightly bitter this time.

"May I review them?"

"I'd rather you did not. They're private. Don't you need a search warrant to do that?"

Augusto laughed heartily. "Here in Mexico, we don't need no stinking search warrants! But I treat you with respect. All I ask is that you give me your co-operation. Could you do that for me?"

"All right." Noreen handed him the camera and showed him how to review the stored images.

Rick returned from the washroom, rubbing his eyes and looking sleepy.

Oscar, seeing that the *cantinero* had departed, slipped behind the bar and grabbed a full litre of Bacardi.

Rick staggered as he went to sit again at the table. "I feel a bit dizzy," he said. "Must be sun-stroke. Do you mind if I lie down over there for a moment?"

Over there sat a wooden bench, covered with a colourful sarape. Over it, a sign said "Many famous people have sat here. Ernest Hemingway, no." Rick stretched out and rapidly started snoring.

Noreen watched while Augusto reviewed the pictures. She was feeling rather languid, until she realized that he was deleting every one of them.

"Don't do that!" she said, and grabbed at the camera. "That could be valuable evidence for you."

Augusto back-handed her, sending her spinning to the floor, and resumed his task of destroying all evidence.

Oscar, the open rum bottle in his hand, came from behind the bar and helped Noreen back onto her chair. He was starting to slur, and Noreen couldn't follow what he was saying to the policeman. Augusto handed the camera back to Noreen, with all the evidence gone.

"*Cabrón*!" she spat out. She knew the worst insult to any Hispanic male was to call him a cuckold.

Augusto sprang up, went behind her chair, and ripped her blouse and bra down to let her breasts bounce freely while her arms were pinned to her torso.

When Oscar objected to this turn of events, Augusto drew his .38 Special and shot him twice, once in the guts and another in the throat. With his spinal cord severed by the slug, Oscar twitched in a massive spasm, then dropped like a sack of tortilla flour.

Noreen shook off both blouse and bra to free her arms and started on a wobbly run toward the door.

Raising the revolver, Augusto was about to stop her with a bullet, but that would terminate the fun-part prematurely. With a curse, he dropped the weapon on the wood floor and tackled Noreen before she could exit.

Dragging her back and using his cartridge belt to lash her wrists to an iron table-leg, Augusto wondered what Rodolfo Fierro, his legendary hero of the *Revolución* would have done. After one battle, he spent a sporting afternoon shooting 297 prisoners with a pair of Smith and Wesson revolvers. Only three got over the barnyard wall to freedom. When asked how he felt about that massacre, Rodolfo complained that his hands hurt. But the prisoners were all men. He probably would have spared the woman for other sport, and shot her later.

* * *

Rick was roused out of his drugged state by the sound of gunfire. When he'd gone to the washroom, he had deliberately made himself barf up most of the Margarita by sticking a finger down his throat. Still, the residual Ketamine was enough to throw him into a genuine stupor for a few minutes.

Through one eye, he surveyed the room. Noreen's hands were lashed to the table. She was kneeling, face on the floor. Her slacks and panties were pulled down below her knees.

Behind her, the phony cop was kneeling, surveying her bare buttocks and pulling down his pants.

As in a slow-motion dream, Rick remembered an old movie. It was Steve McQueen and Ali McGraw in "The Getaway." Rudy, the wounded baddie, was busy bopping the Veterinarian's wife (played by Sally Struthers) while her bound and gagged husband looked on. The next morning, the Veterinarian hanged himself in the bathroom.

He saw the cop, his penis now rampant, spewing saliva down the cleft of Noreen's buttocks. For a second, Rick wondered which orifice the rapist might target first.

With a roll off the bench, Rick achieved his objective, the Taurus revolver, lying on the floor just one metre from the defunct Oscar. From the prone position, he delivered three rapid shots, thundering out in the confined space of the cantina. Two hit the torso, one hit the face, just above the brown nose. The impact drove the rapist onto his back. His still-erect penis stood out of the nest of black hair like a fleshy flagpole. *Viva la Revolución*!

As he untied Noreen, she said, "Thou shalt not kill. Did you absolutely have to kill him Rick?"

"Yeah. Absolutely. Alive, he'd tell so many lies we'd never get out of prison down here. Do you think you can walk as far as the highway? It's about five hundred metres."

"With your help, Rick, I'd walk five hundred miles."

Before they left La Cántara Llena, Rick used a napkin to wipe all fingerprints off their glasses and the gun. Holding the latter with the napkin by the barrel, he pressed Augusto's dead fingers around the grip, and then let it fall again to the floor.

"That should confuse the hell out of the police. They won't waste much time on this investigation. I bet there won't be many mourners at this guy's funeral."

"We don't report what happened here to the authorities?"

Rick looked at her with bemused exasperation. "Noreen, are you still drug-addled? We're walking out of here to the highway, catching a cab to our hotel, flying home tomorrow, and not breathing a word to anyone. Now see if you can get that blouse buttoned-up and look like a respectable woman, her virtue still intact."

* * *

That night, Noreen came into Rick's bed. They had not been intimate in two years. It was good for both of them.

* * *

CHAPTER SIXTEEN

Rick Amyotte was so busy he wondered how he ever had found time to be a police officer. Since his return from Mexico, he'd given two full sets of firearms training classes, coached two private clients on shotgunning and spent hours making gun-stock adjustments on the twelve-gauge Caesar Guerini over-and-under of one of them. It was an expensive shotgun with nice wood. Rick had to proceed carefully. He was no gun-smith, but he could see that the client needed a higher comb, a shorter length of pull, and just a touch of cast-off. He could coach almost anyone with any standard gun into being an adequate shot at Skeet or Trap. For Sporting Clays, with its infinite variety of angles, speed and presentations, only a customized gun fit would let the client sniff close to the elusive goal of excellence.

And in between all this, he was out with his chainsaw in the bush bordering the swamps where he lived, in the frigid March mornings. Before the sap began to rise in the maples, beeches, oaks and ironwoods, it was a good time to cut and stack next year's firewood. "A man who cuts his own wood is warmed twice thereby", Benjamin Franklin stated. This is still true in the twenty-first century.

Rick was also keeping up his running and weight lifting, and he hadn't had a drop of alcohol since he'd left Mexico. He needed to be in top form to decipher the jihadist evil he and Noreen had discovered brewing there.

La Cime Du Plaisir was most surely headed for Canada. Where and when the horror would strike was a mystery that he was compelled to intercept. With Alberto Golondrino involved, he was convinced that all this was linked to his daughter's murder. Someone would have to pay dearly for that atrocity.

* * *

Noreen Amyotte left the church in Glenburnie and drove west all the way to Highway 38. Her spirits were uplifted; matched by the spring sunshine. The last hymn in the service had been "How Great Thou Art." The new organist and choir-master had brought out the best in the music. It was almost as glorious as the version she had at home, sung by the Welsh baritone Bryn Terfel.

She turned north on Highway 38, and south of the Village of Verona, she found the side-road that led to Rick's home. Rick used to hate that hymn. He said it was groveling before a non-existent deity, hoping vainly for pie-in-the-sky. "God created Man," he used to say, "And then Man returned the favour by creating God."

But Noreen knew there was something there, just beyond the reach of human understanding. Sure, religion was man-made, and imperfect. Some religions, like Jihadist Islam, were horrible. But she could see the good that religion could do to alleviate human suffering. Most men couldn't sense this, least of all Rick.

Practically all the members of the group she worked for were from main-stream religions. Noreen had just been named Executive Director of the Ontario Chapter. The group was to help women, at home and abroad, to rise above the oppressive poverty in which they lived. It was called XX - Potential, the XX being the symbol for the female sex chromosomes.

Her new position also paid her a rather generous government-endowed salary. That was one reason she wanted to see Rick – to tell him his support payments would be far less. The other reason was because she was still half-in-love with him.

A mallard hen and drake settled into a swampy puddle by the road-side. Perhaps they'd mate there, and raise a brood of ducklings. Pussy-willows discretely screened their aquatic boudoir. "Blessed assurance, Jesus is mine," Noreen sang to herself, "Oh what a concept of glory divine..."

As she turned into the lane to Rick's bungalow, she saw him in the sunlight, naked to the waist, like an ancient pagan Viking, skinning a furry beast.

"Hi," she said. "It's a coyote?"

"No. It's a wolf."

"What are you going to do with it?"

"I'll tan the skin and put the carcass a klik over yonder for the bears and buzzards."

"You'd rather have a wolf-skin hanging on your wall than leave a magnificent creature like this to be wild and free?" To her, the naked wolf-corpse looked obscene; sickening.

"No, not on a wall. It would make a good cover for a piano bench. Soft on the butt."

"You don't have a piano."

"Well I know someone who does."

"A foam cushion would do as well. Why do you have to always be killing something? Can't you leave Nature alone?"

"No. I can't. Man's presence on this planet has so warped the natural order of things, we <u>have</u> to manage it." He put his knife on the crude wooden table next to the corpse. "Last winter, when the snow was deep and getting mushy, a pregnant doe was torn apart two hundred metres from here. The wolves ate her unborn fawn first, then, started on her liver and haunches."

"It was probably a dog-pack."

"It was wolves. I heard them howling in the night. Their cry is different from coyotes or even malamutes and huskies. I'm just evening up the score – assisting in the balance of nature."

"But <u>you</u> eat deer. You don't have to. Too much meat is bad for your heart and arteries. You can afford to buy what you need at the IGA."

"Supermarket food? It's full of hormones, antibiotics and unhealthy fat. I'm a lot closer to nature living off game meat and the veggies I can grow organically in my little garden and green-house. You're not getting weird and vegetarian on me, are you Noreen?"

"No," she said, tired of arguing. "I believe in eating healthy, too. I came here because I have some news for you, Rick."

She told him about her position with XX-Potential, and how her salary would cut down his support payments.

Rick thanked her, then said "What are you bunch doing for those poor Mayan women we saw in Mexico?"

"When we were there, I noticed that a lot of the skirts, blouses and even sarapes they sold were made in China. That's ridiculous! Mexico grows its own cotton, and has its own artisans. The women there told me they could use some re-conditioned sewing machines either electric, or the old pedal-powered ones. We're getting them for them. Klaus Gipfel has set-up a branch of Summit Industries in Montreal just to take-in and re-furbish the things."

"That's awfully nice of old Klaus. Any more news on his yacht, La Cime du Plaisir?"

"He claims he has loaned it to his son, Dieter, for a business venture. Dieter told his Dad that he and Abu Tomari are trying to assist new refugees get settled in Canada. Rather than place them in crime-ridden urban centres like Montreal, they are settling in rural villages along both shores of the St. Lawrence. The yacht is used to link-up the various communities and bring in ethnic supplies from time to time."

"If Klaus believes that, he believes in Santa Claus and the Tooth Fairy. He's in on it. Noreen! `Ethnic supplies´ – like Kalashnikovs, cocaine and Ketamine? Has anyone told him about his son's marksmanship up on that flat rock at Tulum?"

"No, we agreed to keep silent. Watch and wait. Have you learned anything else new?"

"No. It's remarkably quiet. Have you talked with Lucy Lam?'

"No. I don't see her. Mom does. I guess you do too."

"Not much lately. What does Karla say?"

"She says you should talk with Lucy's brother, Victor. He's a lecturer in Organic Chemistry at the Royal Military College."

"I thought Victor was a musician – a pianist. He and Lucy used to play duets together."

"He is. Sometimes plays with the Kingston Symphony. Anyway, give him a call, or better, go to see him."

"Why didn't Karla or Lucy simply telephone me?"

"Because you're never home, and you, yourself said your line might be tapped. We can't discuss sensitive issues over the phone.

"Noreen, thanks. I'm not going to rest until we get the bastards who killed Tanya – all of them."

"Neither will I, Rick."

"What, not turn the other cheek? Vengeance is mine, I shall repay, says the Lord?"

"You know very well this isn't about vengeance. It's about justice. We'd both better co-operate to help the Lord bring that about. And don't mock my faith, Rick."

"Just clarifying the issue, Noreen, so we're of one mind."

"I think I know who that wolf skin is for. Happy skinning, Rick."

Noreen drove away without looking back.

* * *

CHAPTER SEVENTEEN

Lucy Lam sat on the piano bench, which was covered by a wolf skin, and leafed through some sheet music. Selecting a tone poem by Franz Liszt, she began to play. Once she got into it, her fingers remembered. She closed her eyes and escaped into the magic of the music. The sound filled her half of a duplex town house, which sat by the marshy shore of the Little Cataraqui Creek.

There was a walkway down there by the Creek, with pallet-like bridges over the mucky areas. In the little time Lucy had off from the Hospital, she'd walk along there, watching the waterfowl, the red-wing black birds, the ospreys, herons, muskrats and otters. These last would burble by in a family group, broaching up and down like furry porpoises. The west side of the creek was closed to development, for on it stood Collin's Bay Penitentiary. It looked like it was inspired by the Hotel Chateau Laurier in Ottawa. It certainly would be less opulent inside. Attached to this prison was Frontenac Institution, a minimum security penitentiary, devoted to agriculture. It was a way of keeping the mostly well-behaved cons out of mischief. And the block of land provided habitat for wildlife, right there within the city limits.

As the last note drifted out through the open window, a Pileated Woodpecker did a rat-a-tat-tat applause. He didn't mind that she'd flubbed a few notes. Her brother, Victor, was the more accomplished musician, but he had more time to practice. No, Lucy had to admit to herself, Victor had always had more innate talent than she did, and his fingers were longer. Like Rachmaninov, he could span a tenth. She could barely reach an eighth.

As she stood up from the piano bench, the wolf skin slipped to the floor. Replacing it, she thought of Rick Amyotte. She hadn't seen much of him since his return from Mexico.

That wasn't altogether his fault. Besides her regular work, Lucy was writing an article for the Journal of Toxicology on the date-rape drugs and their effects. She also was involved in helping a pair of Falun Gong refugees from China. The totalitarian regime there thought their religious observances were subversive, since everyone knows that "religion is the opiate of the masses." The couple were musicians; she a violinist, he a cellist. They had embraced Falun Gong, not so much from a spiritual epiphany, but as a passive resistance to the all-intrusive state.

Warned by friends that their arrest was imminent, they fled to Canada just as the net was about to drop. Once arrested, they would likely be executed, and their corneas, kidneys, livers and hearts sold to the highest bidders for transplants.

It's a cruel world, Lucy knew so well since her profession brought her into daily contact with disease and death. Death comes to us all, but the freedom we seek during our lives is a precious commodity, worth fighting for, she thought.

At least Tanya's gun-totin' grandmother, Karla MacTaggart clearly felt that way. So did her erstwhile son-in-law, Rick Amyotte, Lucy's lover.

She was proceeding cautiously with Rick, however. Lucy knew he was drinking again, yet controlling it well...so far. When he'd given her the wolf skin, he informed her that he realized his marriage to Noreen was truly over. "Noreen's a good person, Lucy," he'd explained, "but we're totally incompatible. Her left-leaning, Jesus-freaky, tree-hugging, Bambi-loving ways clash with everything I am and believe in. We end up sniping at each other, even if we try hard not to. I'll work with her and Karla to solve Tanya's murder, but romantically, Noreen and I are done. Neither of us has the strength to tolerate the faults we see too readily in the other."

"I suspect you are more fond of Karla than you are of her daughter," Lucy had observed.

"Yes, but she's about twenty-five years too old for me. As well, she hates me. I destroyed the marriage to her daughter, you see. But that lady's got guts!"

"Backbone, Rick. Guys have guts. Women have backbone," she'd said. "She does what she has to."

* * *

Rick stopped by the Information Centre opposite Kingston's limestone City Hall. Lucy went in and got a map of the area. Almost all the old buildings in Kingston were of limestone. The rock is plentiful around there. The granite of the southernmost part of the Canadian Shield starts to show up fifty kilometres to the north, scraped bare by ancient glaciers during the last ice age.

Victor had told Lucy to get an idea of the lay-out of the military installations of Kingston before they met after his last class at three o'clock at the Royal Military College.

The map had historical references on the back. "Rick," Lucy said as the drove eastward, "did you know that Kingston was once the capital city of Canada?"

"Yes. Only briefly. It was too vulnerable to invasion from the U.S. after the War of 1812. They moved the capital to Montreal and then Toronto, before Queen Victoria finally settled the matter by choosing Ottawa. It had the advantage of access to the Great Lakes and the St. Lawrence because of Colonel John By's Canal up the Cataraqui River which we're about to cross on this bridge, the LaSalle Causeway. Yet it was safely away from the Yankee threat."

"It says here that three hundred men died building the canal, a lot from malaria. Malaria, here in Ontario in the 1820's?"

"You're the doctor, Lucy. Figure it out. Colonel By had military engineers helping him. Many of these had formerly served in India."

"And they were carrying the Plasmodium parasite in their blood. If they took quinine, they wouldn't be sick with fever, but a mosquito could still pick up the bug, bite another worker, and transmit the disease. How our grand plans topple over some microscopic imp!"

"You're not only a physician, Lucy, you're a philosopher."

"I thought you only admired me for my body, and my sexual expertise."

"Well...that too."

* * *

Victor Lam was no taller than his sister. He wore a brush cut to give the illusion of more height. His hands were huge, Rick noticed when they met and shook.

The photo on the desk showed Victor with his blonde, Caucasian wife and two children. The wife, a flautist, was beautiful; the kids cute – probably talented too, Rick thought.

Just as they were about to sit down, the telephone rang. Victor answered it, and spoke briefly in French.

"Your French is excellent," Rick remarked. "Where did you learn it?"

Victor laughed. "Our mother insisted that the older kids should know four languages – Cantonese, Mandarin, English and French. I was born in Ontario but our parents were from Northern Quebec. I wouldn't have a job here at this bi-lingual college, if I didn't speak English and French."

"My family too", Rick said, "Came from there."

"Oh? Lucy didn't tell me."

"I didn't know. Nobody ever mentioned it to me," Lucy said. "I knew about Karla, of course, but not you."

"It doesn't matter. That's the past. What do you have for us, Victor?" Rick asked briskly.

"Probably nothing. But Lucy told me recently about your daughter's tragic death in New York last year, and that your private investigation into the matter has led you to some Muslim extremists?"

Rick nodded. "Why the map of the military installations?"

"Okay. Let's start with that," Victor said. "You noticed the security here at Royal Military College?"

"Yes. We had to sign in and show some I.D. Is it the same all over?"

"It is since 9-11, but we're beginning to get a bit too lax."

Victor pulled down a map which had been rolled-up on a shelf, next to a hanging Periodic Table of the Elements. He spread it out on the desk. "Here we are at the Royal Military College. It's on the east bank of the Cataraqui, as it spills into Lake Ontario. The only major military site to the west is the Canadian Defense Academy, just across the bridge. North of Highway Two we have a small naval training base – HMSS Cataraqui – and the new Athletic Compound. Further north east on Highway 15 is the Military Hospital. East of here, and south of the Highway is Fort Henry, then Vimy Barracks. North of that is the Firing Range."

"All right," Rick said, "We've got a lot of military stuff clustered around here in a rough ellipse, maybe two to three kilometres east-west along Highway Two, and half to three-quarters of a klik wide. You'd need an awfully big bomb to take them all out. And limestone is pretty tough to penetrate with an RPG."

"What is the prevailing wind here?" Victor asked.

"South west," Rick answered, "but what…"

"Rick, can't you see?" Lucy said. "It's not going to be a bomb. It's some kind of gas, let loose somewhere around the Martello Tower at Fort Frederick and carried by the wind to all these installations! What kind of gas, Victor? You teach Organic Chemistry. What would you pick?"

"Well, what I'd pick isn't relevant. What I think the terrorists might choose is Sarin. It was the nerve gas the Japanese terrorists used on the subway in Tokyo in 1995. It's an organophosphate, readily absorbed from the skin and lungs, and is quite lethal in small quantities."

"All right. So what is your evidence, Victor?" Rick asked.

"Not enough to alert the authorities, I'm afraid. But enough to see if you can help to connect the dots, since you are already well-into a private investigation."

"Connect the dots," Rick said. "It's an expression I use. Go on, Victor."

"Around the first of April, they hired some new civilian employees for the cleaning staff here. One of them, name of Sayyid Surat, cleans my office. For a couple of days, this map disappeared from here. Then it re-appeared, but was rolled-up differently than I usually have it. I started looking around to see if anything else was unusual. A textbook on organic toxins had been moved out of its place on the book shelf. It was put back two down from where I keep it. It's a fairly new book, so I stood it up on its back, thus."

Victor placed the book he mentioned on the desk as vertical as he could and let it fall open.

"Someone has flattened that book to photo-copy the pages there," Rick said.

"Exactly. The pages that describe the chemical formula for Sarin and how to make it. Only bad guys want to know things like that."

"Or Chemistry Professors," Rick said. "Anything else you noticed, Victor?"

"Two other things. I got chatting with Sayyid Surat. He said he was born in Quebec, but his accent sounds like the French they speak in North Africa, say Egypt, Tunisia, Algeria or Morocco."

"Sayyid Surat," Rick repeated. "I think that was one of the names on some fake Quebec birth certificates I discovered in Mexico."

"The U.S. forces have not yet captured Osama bin Laden," Lucy said. "Just last week it was reported that he threatened to strike again at the Great Satan and any nation that assisted the U.S.A. I guess that would include Canada."

"I thought so too," Victor said. "And this site seems to be a prime target, more for its propaganda value than anything."

"You mentioned two things," Rick said. "Is that the second?"

"No. the second is something I noticed last week here. It was a yacht, cruising in meaningless circles, where the Cataraqui joins Lake Ontario and the St. Lawrence – just off Fort Frederick."

"An ideal place to release nerve gas if the wind is right. It would do the most damage on a sunny day, with people all outside, would it not?" Rick asked.

"You got it." Victor said. "The RMC Graduation Ceremony is in ten days!"

They sat in stunned silence for a minute.

"Did you catch the name of that boat?" Rick asked.

"La Cime du Plaisir, out of Montreal."

* * *

CHAPTER EIGHTEEN

He was knee-deep in the swamp behind his house. His passage raised up bubbles of smelly marsh gas from the bottom, and silenced the racket of the spring peepers. He was half-expecting trouble, and was armed with his Colt .45 ACP on his hip.

Suddenly, the light faded amongst the dead trees. As if on a signal, bull frogs began their basso chorus in two-part harmony – Jug-o'-rum. Or, as their name says in French – Oua-Oua-ron.

He drew his pistol, and soon knew why. Scores of masked Islamist terrorists, all wearing the checked keffiyeh and carrying Kalashnikovs materialized out of the dark miasma. They were too many for him. Their bullets buzzed like angry hornets around him, miraculously missing. Then, in slow motion, a rocket-propelled-grenade was heading straight for his torso. He couldn't twist out of the way. His feet were mired in swamp muck.

Rick awoke, gasping for air, just a second before the RPG was about to blast him to eternity. He fumbled in the dark, knocked over his alarm clock, and found the scotch. He drank straight from the bottle, about two ounces. It would be enough to help him get back to sleep – settle his nerves. Maybe.

Before dawn, Rick's dreams took him to the parade square at RMC. People in white suits and gas masks walked like specters amongst the scores of dead. They began stacking them up like cord-wood. There were soldiers and cadets, of course, but civilians too, some of them children. Rick cried out an anguished "No!"

The specters turned and came toward him. He, too, would be piled-up with the corpses. He was choking to death.

Rick stumbled out of bed and barely made it to the bathroom before he puked. Tough guy, eh?, he thought as he brushed his teeth, swished, and then gulped some water, hoping it would stay down.

Grasping the bottle of scotch by the neck, he took it to the kitchen and poured it down the sink. He did the same with an almost-full bottle of Barbados Mount-Gay rum. He knew it was easy to vow to remain sober when you're hung-over and frightened. Would he have the guts to stick with his decision? Once again, he had proved the obvious. Controlled drinking never works for an alcoholic.

He dressed quickly and put on the same running shoes he'd been wearing in the swamp, in his dream. He went outside. The dawn was streaking the eastern sky with rose and gold hues. An owl hooted, asking a question, then answering it. The spring peepers did pause in their chorus, but only for a moment. The air was fresh and clean.

Running down the deserted gravel road, Rick had some Chinese music he'd heard on the radio playing in his head. He did not like most Chinese music. He forced his brain to switch to The Steel Rail Blues. It was about some useless twit who gambled away his only ticket to take him home to his beloved. But the beat was good for running.

Still, his guts were so on fire, he had to veer off twice into the bushes for a pit stop.

* * *

Lucy Lam's dream had Chinese music in it. It was part of her heritage, though she preferred the European classics. The dream seemed as in the movie, "Crouching Tiger, Hidden Dragon." Like in the movie, Lucy could defy gravity; do feats of Kung-Fu fighting like she'd never been able to do in the dojo. But in the end, after she had vanquished all the bad guys single-handedly, she came across a trash heap of broken bamboo. On it lay the body of Rick Amyotte, cribillated by a hundred Arab bullets. He had a .45 in one dead hand and a bottle of scotch in the other.

* * *

It was a familiar nightmare for Karla MacTaggart. She was in a shopping mall somewhere, minding her own business, when a policeman approached and asked to examine her purse. "Not without a warrant, or due cause," she said. Then the dream took a different course. The policeman turned into Abu Tomari. He took her to his office, which was in a limestone penitentiary.

When they arrived, she was surprised to see Dieter Gipfel and Alberto Golondrino sitting there. The latter was leering at her. "Let us now see what you have in your purse, Karla", he said, reaching out toward her.

Ripping open the Velcro closure on the split-purse, she grasped her Browning Hi Power in one hand, swept off the safety, and began squeezing the trigger, pointing directly at his mocking, Mexican-Arab face. The damn gun wouldn't fire. He kept laughing at her as she woke up. She was drenched in sweat from a hot flash.

After breakfast, Karla drove in her Subaru to her store in Tweed. The drive took only ten minutes. She went directly to the basement of Next To Nature; unlocked the heavy steel door and turned on the light and the exhaust fan.

After clipping a fresh cardboard target to the hanging frame, Karla ran it down the twenty-yard tunnel with a manual pulley. The range had a dirt backstop. It had been hand-dug by her late husband, Jim, many years before the Attorney General of Ontario became so fussy about range construction. Karla still used it occasionally for testing of some of the firearms she sold. It was less bother than driving to the Tweed Rifle Club.

Using her best ear protection and safety glasses to guard against flying brass, Karla emptied two magazines into the target. The Browning functioned perfectly. With a firm two-handed grip, it was controllable and accurate.

Brownings being easier to strip down than the .45 Colt – designed by the same man, John Moses Browning – she quickly dismantled the handgun and cleaned it with a kit she kept in the drawer of the old table which also served as a firing stand.

The cartridges she replaced in the two magazines were 115 grain, metal-jacketed hollow points, ten in each.

As she emerged from the basement, the pistol safely locked and loaded and nestled in her split-purse, Karla's two employees were just arriving at the store. Fishing was big at this time of year. Rods, reels, lures, hip waders, canoes, boats and motors were selling well.

"You'll have to manage without me for a few hours," she informed them. "I have to go to Kingston. I'll leave my cell phone on. Call me if you have any problems."

Her first stop would be at the Tomari Pharmaceutical Warehouse in Napanee. The hormone replacement pills she had been taking were getting too weak. She had asked her doctor to prescribe a trans-dermal skin cream containing a personalized blend of the correct balance of bio-identical estrogens, progesterone, and a hint of testosterone. This last was to build strength, make her tough – maybe even sexy, though that part of her life had been over for a long time.

Omar Tomari was the only compounding pharmacist between Toronto and Ottawa. He had agreed to make up the prescription for Karla in his laboratory, contained within his warehouse.

After that, she was to go on to Rick Amyotte's bungalow near Verona. That was where they were to meet to plan how to deal with the crisis.

Rick's place was to be the War Room. At last, Karla had gotten all of them working together. There was a chance that her grand-daughter's death would be avenged.

* * *

CHAPTER NINETEEN

Clacking rhythmically, the wiper blades swept the torrents of water and the squished blackfly corpses off her windshield. If this rain kept up, the guests wouldn't be sitting outside on lawn chairs. It would be cramped in Rick's living room. At first, Noreen had refused to come to this meeting, but her mother convinced her otherwise. Karla was right, Noreen knew. If it helped to bring her daughter's murderers to justice, she'd be there, if only to convince Rick not to screw it all up with his trigger-happy, macho *mierda de toro*.

When she turned into Rick's driveway, the rain was abating; the gray sky lightening. Trilliums bordered the gravel, mainly white, the others like they'd been dipped in burgundy. They would fade in another week or so. So would the pesky blackflies, which were voracious up here in the bush where Rick chose to live.

Noreen could see only two other vehicles in the driveway – Rick's and Lucy's. She looked at her watch. She was five minutes late. Where was her Mom? Karla MacTaggart prided herself on promptness and reliability.

The last spurt of the downpour renewed itself just as Noreen exited her car. Despite her sprint to the screen door of the porch, she was unreasonably drenched by the time she came in.

Rick was ready for her with a towel and a mug of coffee with boiled cream, the way she always liked it. Noreen was guided into the living room, and introduced to Lucy's brother, Victor Lam, whom she had not yet met.

A coffee table squatted in the centre of the room, with home-baked bread, fresh-churned butter and local honey, as well as coffee, cream and maple syrup. A pot of green tea perched on a warming plate, with a saucer of sliced lemon beside it. Chairs ringed the table and extended into the corners. The stereo was playing softly in the background. It was Mozart. This was a side of her Ex that Noreen had obliterated from her memory. Or was it all arranged by Lucy Lam?

"Karla called to say she was on her way," Rick explained. "Let's get started anyway. We'll bring her up to speed when she gets here."

As usual, Noreen thought, Rick puts himself in charge and starts using stupid, old cop clichés. Up to speed, indeed. But he was the host. She sat down in a soft armchair and drank her coffee.

"We know only a few facts for sure," he said. "The yacht – La Cime du Plaisir – that Noreen and I saw in Mexico with a bundle of what had to be contraband is here in the Kingston area. Yesterday, it was moored at the Rideau Marina. That is less than two kliks from RMC, where Victor suspects a terrorist attack is about to take place.

"We know four of the people involved in this. Two are in this area right now – Dieter Gipfel and Abu Tomari. Alberto Golondrino, also known in Mexico as Iqbal Ghali Ruíz, was in New York last year, maybe involved in the 9-11 attack, and certainly involved in Tanya's murder. He was in Montreal a week ago, but could turn-up here in a flash. Mahmoud Khalid was instrumental in getting the contraband from South America to Mexico, but hasn't been seen in these parts.

"The only other thing that is certain is that a fifth suspect, Sayyid Surat, a cleaner at RMC, is interested in the military installations in Kingston, and in the nerve gas, Sarin. He has documentation of Canadian birth, but Professor Victor Lam, here, says his French sounds more North African than Québecois. It's also public knowledge that Osama bin Laden has threatened an al-Qaida attack against those who assist the Great Satan. Of the five people I've mentioned, four are Muslims. Only Dieter Gipfel is not of the faith of Muhammad, unless he's had a secret conversion."

"That's all we know for sure?" Noreen said. "Come on, Rick, you saw those fake Quebec birth certificates in their room in Mexico, with instructions as to how to poison people with Ketamine, the drug found in our daughter's body! And that was what spiked our drinks in Mexico. We know that for sure!"

"Yes. Sorry, Noreen. And I think one of the names on those dozen fake passports was Sayyid Surat, but I can't be sure. It certainly leads to a lot of speculation, but surely not enough evidence to take to the authorities."

"It might be helpful," Victor Lam observed, "to speak about our speculations too, so long as we recognize them as such. Lucy, you have itemized our thinking on this."

Yeah, right, Noreen thought. Give Rick's new squeeze – Doctor Dragon Lady – a chance to strut her stuff. But she kept quiet as she got herself a slice of bread and honey and poured more hot coffee into her cup.

Lucy had some jottings listed on a note-pad in her purse but didn't need it for reference. "We suspect that the phony birth certificates have translated into Canadian passports, and a dozen Islamist terrorists, Sayyid Surat amongst them, are now in Canada. We suspect that the contraband seen in Mexico is cocaine, used to finance an al-Qaida strike, and transported here on La Cime du Plaisir We suspect that Sergeant Milos Novak of the OPP Pen Squad could be involved. Less likely, but not entirely ruled-out, are two others – the owner of the yacht, Klaus Gipfel, and Abu Tomari's father, Omar. Those are the personalities we suspect.

"The proposed action is even more speculative. It could be almost anything – a bomb dropped on a nuclear reactor, a suicide plane flown into the dam at Cornwall to flood all of Montreal, an explosion to take down the CN Tower in Toronto, a hit on one of the gas or oil pipelines coming from the west, a blast at one of the major Hydro generators – Niagara or even Northern Quebec. But the most imminent seems to be a nerve gas attack around the Royal Military College. The ideal time for maximum dramatic impact would be the Graduation Ceremonies, and that is less than a week away. But we need more evidence!"

"Yes," Noreen agreed. "We can't stop this alone."

"We might," Victor offered, "alert the military, anonymously of course, so they could be prepared for any such attack."

"Don't you dare!" Rick said. "If we are there trying to foil the action, we'd be the first to get scooped!"

"All this talk, whether fact or fantasy, brings us no closer to apprehending Tanya's murderer," Noreen observed.

"That's what I'd like to do too," said her mother, Karla, from the doorway. "Sorry I'm late. There is someone here I think we need to hear from."

Behind her stood Omar Tomari, father of Abu, the terrorist.

* * *

CHAPTER TWENTY

Omar Tomari, tall, slim, with delicate, pill-counting fingers, stood in the small living room of Rick's home and addressed the seated group.

"Please excuse my interruption. I am here to offer my assistance, slight though it may be, to your cause. I don't know any of you, except for Karla MacTaggart. She and I have a professional association. I am a Pharmacist. But she was asking subtle questions of me about my son, Abu, and I suspected her motive was more than friendly chatting. She did not tell me much – this I hasten to assure you. When I confronted her obvious desperation, she told me only that a suspected Islamist Jihadist attack might be imminent, and Abu was involved. She also said that some people – you I assume – are about to interrupt this attack. I said I'd help in any way I can."

"We'll accept any help we can get, Mr. Tomari," Noreen said. "Please have some tea or coffee, sit down, and we'll listen to you. "I'm…"

"No, no! At this point I don't want to know your names. You may trust my sincerity more in this fashion. But I shall accept your offer of a seat and some coffee."

Once settled, Omar continued. "You may want to know something about your enemy in this. Most western people know that Islam rests upon the divine revelations by God to the Prophet Muhammad fourteen centuries ago, that he wrote these down in a book called the Qur'an, or Koran, if you will. What you may not know, and what many Muslims don't realize, is that Muhammad himself never declared this to be God's last word to humanity. It was almost two centuries before a succession of *khalifas* or Deputies of The Prophet, declared the Divine revelations immutable and literal.

"Just as the Christian religion has its divisions of Catholic, Greek Orthodox, Protestant, Fundamentalist, Jehovah Witnesses, et cetera, Islam, too, has its sub-sects. The Sunnis and the Shi 'a are two well known ones. The Sufi's tend to be mystics, a bit like your Pentecostals. These schisms took place mainly during the seventh century of the common era.

There is one notable exception. Muhammad ibn 'Abd al- Wahhab lived in Arabia during the eighteenth century. He was a fundamentalist, bent on purifying Islam. With the rise of the power and influence of the House of Saud, his particular brand of religious fanaticism has found resonance with the impoverished and down-trodden Muslims of the world.

"Not all Muslims, however, embrace Wahhabism. But unlike Christianity, there are very few secular Muslims. If you are Muslim, Islam defines almost every aspect of your life, your culture and your thought. So Muslims are much more dedicated to their religion than the majority of so-called Christians, and are reproducing at four to five times the rate of the non-Muslim world.

"You have heard the term *jihad*. It means holy war. It can also mean a personal struggle for enlightenment. Muhammad was a warrior and a statesman as well as a religious leader, who enjoined his adherents to wage *jihad* against the enemies of Islam.

"Now comes a fine point. Are Europe and the Western world, with their great democratic traditions and freedom of religion for all, enemies of Islam? No! Even the State of Israel has Islamic members of the Knesset. If Islamic nations or people attack the West, of course they fight back for self preservation. They are fighting an aggressor, not a religion per se.

"Unfortunately, people are as they are, not as we would wish them to be. Most folks are neither deep thinkers nor moral philosophers. They are subject to demagogues and, in the case of Islam, inflammatory, charismatic jihadists.

"I, myself, was sickened by the attack on the World Trade Center. The Qu'ran allows an attack against those who would destroy Islam. But also condemns the killing of innocents, of women and children. It forbids the torture and killing of prisoners. It decries suicide. A *shahid*, or martyr is someone who dies honourably in battle, not some deluded suicide bomber. These bloody acts we are witnessing in the name of Islam are far from a reflection of the true faith."

Omar took a sip of his now-cold coffee.

"That is very illuminating," Rick said. "It may prove helpful. But more pressing is where your son, Abu fits into this historical-cultural scenario. Is he a fanatical jihadist or a rational, moral being like yourself?"

"I wish I knew for sure," Omar replied, shaking his head sadly. "A couple of years ago, two men came to our mosque to lecture. One was Iqbal Ghali Ruíz, also known as Alberto Golondrino. The other was a Saudi millionaire named Mahmoud Khalid. Despite their worldliness, they were Wahhabis and urged our members to return to what they described as the pure faith, and be prepared to wage war against the host society, for its corruption was destroying Islam. By corruption they meant pornography, abortion, alcohol, public nudity and the suffrage of women. The Kingston mosque rejected them, but for the wrong reasons. They did not condemn their proposed murderous attacks on the innocents. No, they became aware that these guys were homosexuals, and kicked them out for that. Wahhabism does not tolerate homosexuals." Omar cleared his throat and paused. His slim fingers trembled as he held his coffee cup.

Noreen asked, "Can you tell us any more about this millionaire Arab, Mahmoud Khalid?" She turned to Rick. "Would it really jeopardize our position if we told Omar?"

"Let me," Rick said. "Omar, there is some association we have discovered between Mahmoud Khalid, Alberto Golondrino, Dieter Gipfel and Abu Tomari. That is all we can say for the moment. Can you, or will you enlighten us?"

Omar put his cup down. "I was trying to keep much of my personal circumstances out of this, but I'm convinced that full candor will perhaps give us a chance to abort a tragedy. Yes, I know more about Mahmoud Khalid.

"My late wife, Miryam, insisted that Abu go to Pakistan to attend a *madrasa* or Islamic religious school. We could afford it, and I thought it harmless, and at least he'd learn more about Islamic culture, history and tradition than we elders at the Kingston Mosque could teach him. It would also improve his Arabic, which might prove useful in his career in Law and Security. Well, he learned more than we'd expected. He learned hatred of all those who do not espouse Islam – the Infidels; you people. He learned all the sneaky tricks the fanatics use against the Jews, the nation of Israel, and any supporters thereof, especially the United States of America. One of Abu's jihadist teachers was Mahmoud Khalid.

"But Khalid was not openly gay in that setting. He could not be, for homosexuality is condemned, even though Muslim men can be seen holding hands and even kissing in public. However, he is an expert at detecting young men who may be confused about their sexual orientation. He encouraged intimate acts between the youths and called it comradeship and bonding, then threatened to expose them if they did not do his bidding. Abu was one of these youths. Some of his companions at the *madrasa* have already blown themselves up in disgusting suicide-murders.

"When Abu came back from Pakistan, shortly before the atrocity in New York, he was full of jihadist zeal. I think the attack had a sobering influence, for he had studied, even memorized the Qu'ran, and he knew that some of the imams were preaching false doctrine. Abu also realized in his heart that he is gay, and wondered how he could fit-in with a religion that would keep him forever in the closet.

"Miryam and I split up for more reasons than I need to elaborate upon. Abu went to visit his mother at Crow Lake, where she was living. He brought along his lover, Alberto Golondrino. I suppose that Miryam had to admit to herself that our son is gay, a sexual orientation condemned by our religion. Miryam was in ill health and mentally unstable at that point. I think this revelation triggered a psychotic episode. She was torn apart by black bears!"

Omar buried his face in his hands.

The rest of them sat in respectful silence.

After he regained some composure, Omar continued. "In my estimation, Alberto Golondrino, aka Iqbal Ghali Ruíz is a psychopath and a fraud. He is no longer Abu's lover, Dieter Gipfel <u>is</u>, I believe, and is the same person who shot Miryam in the leg! Ironic, isn't it? Dieter shoots Abu's mother, goes to prison, Abu becomes his Case Management Officer and later his lover. And now they may be co-conspirators in something – that you are trying to stop.

"But I plead with you for one thing. I know Abu. Misguided he may be, but he's not totally bad. If he does wrong, then he must pay and be brought to justice. Justice, yes, I plead for that. But please don't kill my son!"

* * *

CHAPTER
TWENTY ONE

"**A** lively discussion followed", as the reporters say of the meetings of the South Frontenac Council. In Rick's swamp-surrounded rural bungalow, it did not take long for their amateur anti-terror task force to become mired in the muck.

Omar Tomari suggested he could manufacture some LSD to confuse the jihadists. Lucy Lam, the toxicologist, thought it would be an effective chemical, rendering the recipients temporarily insane. Yet the dose was difficult to calculate, uncertain in its delivery, and the reaction of already-insane jihadists totally unpredictable.

Rick pointed-out that the enemy would be well-trained with a variety of weapons, whereas only he and Karla MacTaggart had skills with firearms.

Victor Lam asked Omar, the pharmaceutical entrepreneur, if he could supply them with a dozen 400 millilitre glass bottles with rubber stoppers, perforated with a hole four millimetres in diameter. He explained that he had access to a few five-second fuses at RMC, and that naphtha, readily-available as camp-stove fuel, is highly volatile. Any amateur could be armed with an effective Molotov cocktail thereby.

Rick agreed that such grenades would even the odds a bit, but would be not much defense against Uzis, Kalashnikovs and RPG's.

"However, I propose that I scout out the area around the marina further, and we hit the bastards with whatever we have the night before the graduation ceremony. An extra-judicial, pre-emptive strike is far more effective than the shillyshallying around that the authorities would do,"

The air in the living room was thick with electric tension. No one spoke for a full minute. The enormity of this scheme, its implications, the possibility of failure, the legal consequences all tumbled through their minds.

Finally Noreen broke the silence. "There is, I believe, a psychiatric diagnosis called *folie-à-deux*. Am I correct in this, Dr. Lam?"

Lucy nodded. "Yes. It's usually a paranoid delusional condition where a dominant member of a household insists that at least one other buys into the delusions."

"And there could be more than one?" Noreen asked, "Like the poor people who drank poisoned Kool-Aid at Jonestown, Guyana?"

"Or like the brain-washed suicide bombers who think they'll go directly to paradise and have eternal access to seventy lascivious virgins," Lucy answered. "That would be, I suppose, folie-à-beaucoup."

Rick interrupted. "All religions are delusional. They ask you to believe literally in a story which is merely allegorical or mythical. What's your point, Noreen?"

Karla spoke up. "She has a point, Rick, and it's a good one. We are all following your lead here, accepting as fact too many things that are only speculative and could be dead wrong. Then we, and many others, could end up both dead and wrong."

"Exactly!" Noreen said. "Rick, you are so convinced that the powers of the state are either malignant or ineffectual, that you are ready to ride-out, like the Lone-fucking-Ranger, and commit a worse atrocity than you're trying to prevent. You're asking us to support you in that. Well as much as I, too, want to catch our daughter's killers, I'm not with you on this. The state has enormous resources and intelligence that we don't. We could have working for us, all the wisdom and strength of the Military, the Coast Guard, the Kingston Police, the Ontario Provincial Police, the RCMP, even the U.S. Coast Guard and the FBI for God's sake. All we have to do is make them aware of our concerns, pool our resources, and let them handle it!"

"Noreen, I've been a cop! Let them handle it? It would be an enormous cluster-fuck! This operation calls for a selectively precise strike, not what you'd get from all these law-enforcement groups. Besides, we only have four days. Of course I'll do what I can to glean more information before we move. But keep the cops and the army out of it. It would only complicate matters."

"Why don't you all vote on it?" Omar Tomari suggested. "I, of course, as a visitor here, would abstain."

"Vote on it?" Rick roared. "General, please, could we have a vote to decide whether we should attack the enemy?" The last was spoken in a mocking falsetto.

"That's the trouble here, Rick," Karla said. "I admire your strength and especially your defense of individual rights. I, too, mistrust the obtuse powers of the state, with good reason. But you have assumed a leadership here that is not warranted."

"He always does," Noreen said. "John Wayne and Charles Bronson are his two favourite actors. Death Wish, True Grit and the Magnificent Seven –

he's seen each movie ten times. Macho-cowboy-hero-idiot! Well I'm not staying around here a minute more. Do what you have to, Rick, and I'll do what I have to!" She started for the door.

Lucy went after her. She paused in the door frame, her slim figure silhouetted by the sunshine outside. "I'll do what I can to help Noreen calm down. But she's right, Rick. This time, she's right, and you are wrong."

"*Et tu, Brute?*" Rick replied.

"Quote Shakespeare's Julius Caesar if you like. Call this treachery if you will. But blind loyalty is always trumped by the truth."

Then Lucy Lam and Noreen Amyotte were gone.

The others filed out slowly after them, leaving Rick alone.

* * *

CHAPTER TWENTY TWO

Alone at last, Rick thought.

The unaccustomed babble and dissention in his home had given him a headache. "I don't get headaches; I give them", he used to joke. Well now he had one, and he wished there were some booze in the house to relieve his misery, albeit temporarily.

His worst fear in this was about to happen. Noreen was determined to stop him. She was already pals with one conspirator, Klaus Gipfel, who was rehabilitating old sewing machines for her XX- Potential Aid Agency. And she'd always been friendly with Milos Novak, who had been most consoling to her after Tanya's death. But Milos had deliberately covered up things Rick needed to know, and his sudden wealth and association with Abu Tomari and Dieter Gipfel spelled only one thing – drugs. He <u>had</u> to be in on that bale of cocaine shipped into Canada. As a Sergeant in the Pen

Squad, he was well-positioned to protect the drug-dealers of his choice, both inside and outside the Joint, and clamp down on any competition. Noreen would turn to him, and Milos would be sure to find some pretext to get Rick arrested before he could act.

It's amazing how clear your mind becomes when you know you are soon to be hanged, he thought. He looked out the doorway at his eight-year-old Isuzu Trooper, glistening green in the spring sunshine, a few sparse raindrops sparkling like diadems. With a bundle of newspapers and masking tape, Rick covered the door handles and the windows of the boxy vehicle. He noticed the old stone chip low on the left windshield, and was satisfied that the crack had not spread more than a few centimetres.

His only paint was a gray, exterior enamel house paint. At least it was oil-based. The bucket was three-quarters full, but gunky. Judiciously adding paint thinner and stirring vigorously, Rick got it liquid enough to work in his sprayer without clogging it. The damn vehicle would have to be properly re-painted, but at least for now it would be gray, not green.

Once finished the spray-painting, Rick removed the tape and paper and left the Isuzu to dry in the sunshine. In his garden shed, which once had been a chicken coop, he found two old Ontario license plates. Since the stickers were eight years out of date, Rick was about to manufacture new ones to glue on, when he saw that the old colours were the same as this year's. Only a close inspection would reveal their antiquity.

As he exchanged the plates, Rick's chest tightened in sorrow and rage over the defection of Lucy Lam. He'd thought that he could count on her, above all others. But like rats deserting a sinking ship, they'd all fled, even Lucy. Worse, she had sided with Noreen, against him. It seemed to him like the ultimate betrayal, that of a lover. He was going to miss her tenderness, her comfort, her sexuality.

As he wrenched in the last bolt on the plaques, he thought, well, screw her! Better to have nobody than a treacherous viper at my breast.

In the next two hours, as the vehicle dried in the sun, Rick stuffed a travel shaving kit and some underclothes and shirts into a duffel bag. He added his camouflage turkey-hunting jacket, pants, cap, mask and gloves.

Then, looking to his armament, he selected his Colt .45 ACP. With one round in the chamber and seven in the magazine, he'd have eight shots, each one a man-stopper. He stuffed the semi-auto into an inside-the pants holster on his right hip, and put three spare loaded magazines into his left trouser pocket.

His .308 calibre deer rifle would hold five rounds. Rick packed the whole box of twenty cartridges.

Removing the magazine plug from his Remington pump action 12 gauge, Rick could carry five buckshot loads in it. He took three boxes of five each and put them into the butt-end of the canvas camo gun case. As an after-thought, he hooked a Buck folding clip knife on his belt. Don't take a knife to a gun fight, he thought, but you never know.

He wished he had his old police flak vest, but that was OPP property.

He was as prepared as he could be, except for two things. He was short of information, and short of time. He'd have to neutralize the bad guys before the cops rushed in to screw it up.

But where, and how?

* * *

CHAPTER TWENTY THREE

It was evening, the sun setting blood red across the Cataraqui River over Kingston when Rick checked into the motel on Highway 15. The location was perfect – close to the Rideau Marina, and less than a kilometre from the elliptical congregation of the military installations he'd seen on the map in Victor Lam's office at RMC.

At the liquor store, Rick had not spotted Victor Lam when he bought a mickey (the U.S. calls it a pint) of Wild Turkey Kentucky Bourbon. Rick had failed to get a wild turkey that spring, but he could at least drink some in consolation. Sippin' whiskey. It would be all right so long as he didn't sip too much. Dutch courage.

As he paid for his two bottles of table wine, Victor Lam watched Rick getting into his gray Isuzu. He followed Rick to the motel and called his sister, Lucy, with this information.

* * *

Lucy Lam sat in her car in a mini plaza and kept an eye on the motel. She had thought about going in and reasoning with Rick, but knew it would be useless. He was as stubborn as a male dog tackling a porcupine. No matter what the consequences, he'd do the manly thing and probably get himself killed. The best she could do was to hover in the background and call for help if his actions became critical. Lucy was armed only with her cell phone.

When the gray Isuzu 4X4 passed the plaza, Lucy had to drive a discreet distance behind, for she knew Rick would be wary. There was enough traffic so that her headlights would not be obvious to him in the darkness.

Once she saw where he was parking, Lucy drove on. She knew she'd find him in one of the bars in the Hub, at Princess and Division.

It was half an hour later and the second bar she tried when she saw him. Slipping a five to the doorman, Lucy stood and watched Rick drink a beer, then get up and dance with a flaming red-head.

It wasn't her best choice of colour, Lucy thought. She's not fat, but certainly what they call voluptuous. She'll be fat in a year or so unless she works out.

"Who is that red-head in the green turtle-neck?" she asked the doorman.

"Which red-head? Oh, her. Last week she was a blonde. Her name is Dorothy, but everyone calls her Doll. I dunno her last name. Comes in here once or twice a week. Likes to dance. Doesn't seem to have a steady, right now anyway."

"Thanks," Lucy said. "She looks just like my cousin, but it's not the same person. Which way to the washroom?"

The doorman directed her. When Lucy came out, both Rick and Doll were gone. She checked for his vehicle. It was gone too.

Lucy went home feeling lonely and sick.

* * *

CHAPTER
TWENTY FOUR

C lad in his Realtree camo, with a face mask, and hidden by brush, Rick Amyotte was virtually undetectable. He was on the east bank of the Cataraqui River, just south of the bridge where Highway 401 crossed it. From there through the bushes, he had a clear shot along the newly-made path from the motel, right down to the river, where Freddy Gagnon said La Cime du Plaisir tied up. In his .308 bolt action were 150 grain pointed soft points, and his variable scope was cranked up to seven power. He could knock the nuts off a gnat at two hundred metres.

Freddy Gagnon was a river rat. Mostly, he lived in a tar-paper shack on some abandoned land and supported himself with fishing, trapping and collecting beer bottles and cans for return to the Brewer's Retail Store. They were worth ten cents apiece. When it got really cold, like below minus fifteen Celsius, Freddy would slap a friendly cop on the shoulder.

The constable would explain to the Justice of the Peace and the Crown Attorney that it had been a minor "assault" and arrange for Freddy to spend the next few weeks in Quinte Regional Detention Centre until the weather warmed up. The cop, the Justice, the Crown, the Magistrate and the jailers at Quinte all knew it was a charade, calculated to save Freddy from freezing. They never let on though, not even to each other. Justice must be not only fair, but seen to be so.

Rick couldn't find Freddy Gagnon at first. That is why he went to the Hub, to find Doll, Freddy's sister. From her, he learned that Freddy had been at the Sally Ann shelter because someone had stolen his cook stove. That very day, an employee at the Brewer's Retail gave Freddy a propane camp stove and he'd just moved back into his shack.

When Rick found Freddy, he learned that La Cime du Plaisir was docking in a large beaver channel amidst the cat-tails just below a motel on Highway 15, south of 401. Freddy noticed such things. For this, Rick rewarded him with the mickey of Wild Turkey Kentucky Bourbon. He probably should have given him cash, but that would have been an insult. Freddy was none-too-bright, and Rick hated to pickle the few functioning neurons, but bourbon was Freddy's favourite and he was generally a quiet drunk. Besides, it removed the temptation from Rick's six-pocket camo pants.

The sky was the colour of a lead bullet. The wind was from the east, behind him – a warm wind. It would rain soon. Rick shifted his rifle to slap a mosquito that was brave enough to penetrate the layer of DEET on the gap between his face mask on his cheek and his hat. He had nothing to do but wait.

He was feeling mixed about not trying to bed Doll. He never had, although he had danced with her before and bought her the odd drink. Certainly, he was horny enough; deprived of such release for some time now. And she likely could be talked into it. He knew she really liked him. Now deserted by both wife and lover, Rick was a free man. But he'd restrained himself. Why? There was a mutual attraction, and she seemed hetero.

It probably wasn't pure morality. Women get to think they own you once you dip the dinky. Can't blame them – that's just the way they are. They want more than sex. They want commitment. Rick fancied himself an expert lover. Doll would probably fall in love with him. Then, like a dog chasing a car, what did he plan to do with it when he achieved his goal?

As well, he didn't want Doll to discover the locked and loaded .45 on his hip. So he'd driven around with her for a few minutes, learned about Freddy, gave her a brotherly kiss and a twenty, and deposited her back at the Hub so she could troll for more reliable prospects – with more commitment than he had to offer.

Before he'd got into position with his rifle, while he was cruising slowly past the motel, Rick had seen a black Lincoln Navigator pull in there, in front of room 21. It was on the ground floor, south end. When he drove back on Highway 15, the Navigator was leaving, heading south, as he was. That was Abu Tomari's vehicle. Two guys, each with a dark mustache, were hauling a crate of something into the motel together with several oblong bundles. Most of them were the size of Uzis. One was larger, like a bazooka.

Rick had parked at the car-pool lot three hundred metres to the north and worked his way through the brush with his rifle to set-up a sniper blind. All that had taken a good forty-five minutes.

Rick had been waiting in his lair above the river for another half-hour, slapping mosquitoes when he heard a child's voice calling.

"Willi! Willi!" The W was pronounced in the German way, like a V.

He stopped slapping and squirming; made himself still as a rock. There was a faint swish of fur on spring buds. Turning his head slowly, he found himself staring into the pitiless yellow eyes of a large German Shepherd, its ears flattened back, its fangs bared. A rumbling growl rasped from deep in its throat. Rick couldn't move his rifle to bear on the beast. One twitch, and the dog would be upon him ripping his throat, for the canine clearly had been trained to recognize guys with guns as adversaries, to be neutralized as expediently as possible.

"Oh, there you are, Willi," the girl exclaimed, coming up the path Rick's boots had made. Then she saw Rick, and stopped. "Sit and stay, Willi!" She commanded.

Willi did, but still had his fangs bared.

The girl, about six years old, looked carefully at Rick. "Are you a soldier, sir?" she asked.

"No. I'm a hunter."

"What are you hunting?"

"Foxes and coyotes. There are some rabid ones around – crazy animals that bite people and make them sick. Sometimes they die." It wasn't exactly a lie, if taken figuratively.

"Did you shoot any yet?"

"No, not yet. Willi obeys you well. Is he your dog?"

"No, he's my Grand-father's dog. I was supposed to stay in the car, but I had to go pee-pee and Grandpa was taking so long with his business that I couldn't wait. When I opened the door, Willi jumped out. I guess he tracked you here. And I tracked Willi," she said proudly. "The other dog didn't jump out. She's a female. They're smarter, or at least less stubborn than males, Grandpa says."

"Your Grandpa's other dog, is she a German Shepherd too?"

"No, she's all gray. Her name is Treu."

"Um….my name is Richard. What is yours?" Rick was glad to see that Willi was beginning to relax.

"Mona. My Mom went to heaven and my Daddy is away, so I came to live with Grandpa Klaus."

Dieter's kid. Rick didn't know that Dieter had a daughter. "Listen, Mona, you better get yourself and Willi back in the car, so your Grandpa Klaus won't get worried. Don't tell him you saw me here. He might not like you talking with strangers. But if he guesses, just tell him I'm a friendly hunter."

"Oh, he's a hunter too. He'd understand," Mona said. Then she and Willi left, back the way they came.

As Rick returned to his surveillance, he watched two men depositing the heavy box on a wooden pallet that served as a crude dock. They were covering it up with dead reeds from last year's growth. Through his scope, Rick could see one of the men was an Arab with a mustache. The other was Dieter Gipfel.

Dieter lingered on the river bank for a few minutes after the other had returned to the motel. He was looking south, no doubt awaiting the arrival of La Cime du Plaisir. Then he, too, returned to the motel.

This was the first time in his life that Rick had identified a man through a rifle's scope. It was contrary to all he knew about safe gun handling, and what he taught in his classes. And he was tempted to thumb off the safety and squeeze the trigger. But he wanted more than Dieter. He wanted them all.

Pondering what to do next, Rick heard the "vroom" of twin mufflers. Through a tunnel he quickly pawed through the bush on his left, he saw Dieter's maroon Durango pulling out onto the Highway and heading south, no doubt to speed up the arrival of the yacht.

Rick had to find out what was in that crate, and he did not have a lot of time!

* * *

CHAPTER TWENTY FIVE

S cylla and Charybdis – the boulder and the whirlpool. Or nowadays, caught between a rock and a hard place.

Since events were coming together like ravens on road kill, Rick slipped his rifle into the case, left it in the sniper blind and scrambled as surreptitiously as he could down to the river. He hadn't quite made it to examine the crate on the shore, before the two Arabs with Uzis were coming down the path from the motel, while La Cime du Plaisir was churning up-river toward him. Flattening himself into the thickest clump of marsh grass he could find, Rick drew his .45 and waited.

The guys above him stopped, flicked away their cigarette butts and lit fresh ones. The smoking sentries stood there, as the yacht drew closer. A tendril of grass smoke wafted past Rick's nose. God, no! Those idiots had lit the marsh, full of last-year's dried cat-tails, on fire. The flames were licking straight toward Rick's hiding place.

To handle the crisis, the two Arabs started stomping on the flames, and doing a fair job of it. Mercifully, it began to rain, a May shower. The fire stopped just short of Rick's right hand which was grasping the pistol. The flames fizzled out with the downpour.

The closest stomping Saudi turned back a metre from Rick and walked toward his companion, speaking Arabic. They both were unslinging their Uzis.

Rick knew he'd been seen. He rose to a kneeling position and held the Colt in a two-handed grip. The one guy was eight metres away, the other about ten. Rick had about a half a second to hit the nearest centre of mass, double tap the other, then come back to the first to make sure of him. A tactical sequence, it was, as he'd been trained.

A bullet whizzed past Rick's ear, followed by a boom from the hillside above. He was being shot at by his own rifle!

He couldn't stay still – a sitting duck. As in a dream, he got to his feet and began running through the soggy marsh, his boots sinking ankle deep, as if into molasses. But at least he was moving.

The two sentries were momentarily bewildered, not knowing which target to choose first. Rick was the closest. The other had a rifle, but it would be a long shot for a nine-millimetre Uzi. Simultaneously, they chose Rick as their target.

Flinging a quick shot in their direction, Rick pumped his legs frantically, trying to zigzag. Slugs ripped through the reeds around him on all sides. Someone was shooting at him from the yacht as well.

One leg plunged deeply into a hidden hole in the marsh, and Rick went down again, sprawling across a muskrat mound. It knocked the wind out of him, and the .45 flew out of his hand. The fire had burned the weeds around him. He might be screened from the guys in the yacht and the Arabs with Uzis, but the sniper on the hillside had a clear shot at him.

He slid down behind the muskrat mound, tried to sink as low as he could into the swamp, and awaited his fate.

The rifle cracked again and again from the hillside and the lethal messengers of death whizzed around his head, vaporizing the raindrops they encountered on the way.

* * *

CHAPTER TWENTY SIX

Klaus Gipfel lay on his belly, clutching Rick's rifle. He'd had to adjust the scope to his eye, for in the downpour, his glasses were useless. He'd removed the oiled cotton from his ears so he could hear Rick approaching. He knew that he would come upon him from behind.

Thunder crashed, louder than the rifle's report. It was a three second burst. A man could cover a lot of ground in three seconds.

Like a marsh-monster, Rick appeared on his right, his camo outfit covered in rank swamp muck. Smart. It's harder to swing a rifle to your right, especially prone. Klaus lay still, for the .45 was in Rick's hand, his index finger along the trigger guard and his thumb on the safety. Klaus knew that Rick could aim and shoot in a third of a second. "Hello, Rick," he said. "Exciting, *nicht wahr?*"

"Jawohl. I don't know whether to shoot you or hug you. If you were really trying to hit me, you're a lousy shot. But you did manage to drive away the bad guys. They all jumped on board your yacht and headed up river. Did you put any holes in your boat?"

"Wouldn't dream of it. If I'd been trying to hit you, Rick, I could have, at least five times." Klaus worked the bolt and caught the cartridge as it flipped out. He handed the rifle to Rick and stood up. You'll have to re-focus the scope."

A siren sounded on Highway 15, to the south.

"We'd better get out of here," Klaus suggested. Leave your vehicle where it is. My Mercedes is parked closer, at the side of the road over there. I'll get us away from here."

"I'll muddy the upholstery."

"You can sit in the back, on the dogs' blanket. It's washable."

"So long as Willi doesn't want my arm for lunch."

"Ah, so. You've met Willi?"

"And your grand-daughter, Mona. You shouldn't leave her alone like that."

"She's not alone. Willi and Treu are with her. Besides, I checked on her ten minutes ago. She's asleep in the front seat. Now let's skedaddle."

Rick wondered where on earth Klaus had heard such an archaic expression.

* * *

"It's not for Dieter's sake I'm doing this," Klaus stated. They were sitting in the den of his mansion on Fourteen Island Lake. Rick had showered, washed his clothes, and wore one of Klaus' bathrobes while they dried in the machine. They had eaten dinner with Mona, and she'd retired clutching her favourite stuffed teddy bear.

"Then why?" Rick was drinking from a mug of apple juice.

Klaus sipped his *schnapps*. "It's for Mona, poor little thing. I didn't even know she existed until three weeks ago. Then, when her mother died of an overdose of cocaine – supplied by my rotten son, Dietrich – I got a call from some neighbours who had taken Mona in. Either I could go and get her in Montreal, or they would apply to be her foster parents. But they already had two of their own plus one other foster kid. And now, having written-off my own son as an incorrigible psychopath, I'm trying to provide a stable home for her, and minimize whatever damage Dieter is up to."

"Why did you lend him your yacht, La Cime du Plaisir?"

"He told me that some drug dealers were after him. He claimed he had a business deal that would settle the affair and buy-off the contract that was out on him. Psychopaths can be really convincing and persuasive when they want something. He begged me. One last time. 'Don't give up on me, Dad,' he said. I felt a bit better about it to know that Abu Tomari was going with him to Mexico. He was Dieter's Case Management Officer while he was in Bath Institution. He seemed to believe that Dieter was salvageable. Now, I'm convinced not. Dieter has corrupted Abu like everyone else he touches."

"Are they both gay?" Rick asked.

"Abu is. It must be tough for him, being Muslim. Dieter, he's polymorphous. He'll go with whoever strikes his fancy or might be of use to him. I don't know if Abu realizes this yet."

"What about Alberto Golondrino?" Rick asked

"Oh, he's an even slicker psychopath than Dieter. He was in Kingston yesterday. Met with Abu and Dieter. I suspect a lot of money changed hands. He would collect from al-Qaida vast sums for helping to get those

Islamist terrorists their Canadian passports, plus he has a network of drug dealers in Montreal, Kingston and Toronto to unload whatever cocaine Dieter hasn't snorted up his nose personally.

"I've had a pair of private detectives shadowing them for the past four weeks. I don't know what they're planning, but whatever it is, I want to stop it. Dieter has had his last chance. Killing his girl-friend, Mona's mother, even inadvertently, was his last outrage. And the couple who took in Mona showed me correspondence. That's how they found my address and telephone number. That girl truly loved and trusted Dieter. Like me, she believed the pack of lies he lays down wherever he goes."

Klaus drained the last of his *schnapps* in one gulp, and slammed the goblet down on the table beside the wood-duck lamp. "If no one else stops that lying little shit, I will, even if I have to kill him myself!"

* * *

After Rick got dressed in his own clothes, he told Klaus about their suspicions. It looked like it would be nerve gas attack, launched from the yacht by a rocket propelled grenade, and into the Parade Square at RMC during the Graduation Ceremony. With a south west wind, the gas would spread throughout the military complexes there, leaving the terrorists unscathed. And the ceremony would be in forty-eight hours!

"Have you any ideas on how we can stop them, Klaus?"

"You haven't gone to the authorities yet, Rick. Why not?"

"You haven't either. You think it's time? All my allies think we should. They call me a macho cowboy paranoid."

Klaus grinned wryly. "Are you paranoid, or is the State really out to get you? I'm a Canadian citizen, Rick, but I lived under totalitarian Communism throughout my youth. Why did I come to Canada? For freedom. But I asked for no hand-outs from the government. Summit Industries I built up myself with hard work and calculation. And how did the State reward me? By confiscating my firearms for something Dieter did! Canada gives us the <u>right</u> to life, liberty and security of the person, but leaves us stripped of the fundamental right of self-defense! Where did your people come from, Rick? Are you the son of *Voyageurs, Coureurs-de-bois?*"

Rick nodded. "Something like that."

"And the actions of my psychopathic son prompted the State to kick you off the police force. Not politically correct enough? Well I don't trust the bastards either. If you're a macho cowboy paranoid, then so am I."

"Just you and I against the bad guys, Klaus? We'd better have a plan. And it better be a good one."

"I have an idea, Rick, that just might work. And let us not be troubled by what is legal. We need to do the right thing!"

* * *

CHAPTER TWENTY SEVEN

"How long would it take you to drive to your home and back here, Rick?" Klaus demanded. The old German seemed to have assumed command, though it was not specifically discussed.

"I could be back in less than an hour."

"There are a few things we'll need out of your workshop," Klaus explained. "I should be getting back my Possession and Acquisition License for firearms any day now, but so far I've been deprived of primers and powder as well as guns and ammo. Here's what I think we need." He handed over a list of re-loading items.

"I have all these. How about a firearm for you?"

"You can't cart around a rifle and a shotgun too. I'll take the shotgun. I'll need both buckshot and rifled slugs. We'll be working most of the night, and, like in a *Blitzkrieg*, we strike at dawn!"

"I may be just a backwoods-*canadien,* but I'm not budging from here until I can understand what in hell you're planning with your *Blitzkrieg.* I didn't know you were such an admirer of Adolf Hitler."

"I'm not. He was a psychopath too. But you have to admit that Guderian and Rommel were, in their own way, brilliant.

"Briefly, Rick, here's the scheme. While you're gone – take my Mercedes please – I'll be arranging a few things by phone. Of course I'll have to get Mona cared-for. If I had a wife, it would be easier for the tyke. But there's a widow who lives down the road, on Wood Duck Lane. Mrs. Tavares' husband made a fortune in marble tiles and slate. He fell off a roof a year ago, and died. She has met Mona, and would be over here in a instant if I asked her.

"Next I have to locate where the terrorists have hidden my yacht. I suspect it's not at the Marina. One or other of my private detectives can likely tell me, within the hour. It's early yet. Then I have to find a way to get Alberto Golondrino, aka Iqbal Ghali, back here. We might as well make a clean sweep of it!"

Rick could see the fire in the old man's eyes. He was probably as mad as Don Quixote. "I admire your zeal, Klaus, but how are you planning to get Golondrino back here?"

"I'll telephone him. My detectives have a list of his private phone numbers in Toronto and Montreal. He has to be in one of those residences."

"Just like that? You'll speak with him and invite him to join the lads on the yacht so that we can blow them up together? Sounds rather iffy to me! Or will you speak to him in Arabic?"

"No, I don't speak Arabic. I'll tell him the truth."

"The truth. That's just great, Klaus, just great. I'd better go and find a doctor, preferably a psychiatrist to treat your grandiose psychosis."

"Well......not the <u>whole</u> truth. I'll tell him I'm worried about Dieter's stability because of his drug use. 'I know,' I'll say, 'that you are a good friend of both Dieter and that wonderful fellow who helped him so much, Abu Tomari. I think Dieter is going into a manic crisis. He could be dangerous to himself and to others around him. I can't reach Abu Tomari. He seems to have disappeared. Even his father can't tell me his whereabouts. Could you please come and try to help my son before it's too late?' How does that sound, Rick?"

Nodding, he replied, "Better. I'm not completely re-assured that you're not even more psychotic than I am, but it might work. Golondrino would stand to lose a fortune if the operation got scuppered. He'll likely get down here *pronto*."

"*Pronto*, I understand. But scuppered?"

"It's a nautical term, Klaus. You're a yachtsman. Look it up."

* * *

CHAPTER
TWENTY EIGHT

The night should have been exhausting, with all they had to do. But working together, things went slicker than goose grease.

In the cold water of the St Lawrence River in the hours before dawn, Rick and Klaus were paddling in a sixteen-foot aluminum canoe toward Cedar Island.

"She has the hots for you, Klaus," Rick observed. He was in the stern, feeling energized, despite the lack of sleep.

"Mrs. Tavares? I know. She's a nice lady, but not my type. Too fat, too hypochondriac, and too religious for me."

The religious part caused Rick to think of Noreen. People could be nice in their own way; just not suitable as partners.

They paddled in silence for a while. Cedar Island is one of the first of the Thousand Islands in the St Lawrence. It is less than a kilometre from the ancient cannons of Fort Henry, with the Royal Military College lying at the base of Fort Henry Hill.

When they had gone to collect Rick's vehicle, they checked below the Jihadists' motel and found the crate was still there at the secret cove, covered with dried bulrushes. In it were several boxes of 9mm Parabellum ammo, and some 7.62 X 39 rifle cartridges – the calibre of the Kalashnikov. Klaus and Rick had 'special-loaded' some of each calibre that evening. They substituted their own into the top boxes of each. It might help. It might not.

More important was to alter all three of the RPG rounds in the crate. They were only guessing but both men were knowledgeable about gunpowder and ballistics. Working by flashlight, they hoped their alterations would not be noticed. If they could strike the enemy before dawn at Cedar Island, these preparations would be for naught, for their plan was to disable the yacht, call in the authorities, and hope that there would be enough evidence on board to convict all of the conspirators.

"Look what they did to my yacht!" Klaus said. He was peering through a sensitive star-light scope, held in his hands.

Rick swung the canoe broadside and reached forward to grasp the scope.

"Is that your boat, La Cime du Plaisir? The super-structure is yellow now, not white, and the name on the stern says….Delilah. It's the only one moored at the government dock. Are you sure?"

"It's mine all right. They did a worse job of re-painting than you did on your truck!"

"I was in a hurry. So were they. What now?"

They had taken Rick's Isuzu Trooper farther south on Highway 15 after their work on the crate, and caught a couple of hours of sleep at the motel room that Rick had rented. At four a.m., they launched the canoe from the dock of a friend of Klaus who lived on the St Lawrence east of Vimy Barracks.

"We can't do a naval assault. They'd blow us out of the water. Let's go to the west end of the island and attack from the land", Klaus murmured as he paddled.

Kingstonians never seem to know whether the muffin-like, limestone fortifications scattered around are Martello Towers or Murney Towers. Whatever they are called, there is one on Cedar Island, almost identical to the one facing it at Fort Frederick, at RMC. They were built during the War of 1812 to repel an American invasion. The engineers who designed them had the idea that, once a key bolt was removed, one good bash with a sledge hammer on an iron rod would cause the wooden walls to fall away so the cannon would be free to swivel in any direction to bear on the enemy. No one ever had to test the theory in actuality.

Rick was approaching the tower cautiously, for a Great Blue Heron had taken off squawking from the rocky shore as they tied up their canoe. An owl hooted by the tower. Was it an owl, or a signal?

Rick waved to Klaus to circle to the right. Klaus grasped the shotgun. Rick had both his rifle and his .45. The tower was a good two hundred metres from the yacht. Any gunshots would deprive them of the element of surprise and probably end in their death. Two against six or eight or ten were not great odds.

The owl hooted again, and an answering one came from the yacht. Rick stayed still, belly to the ground. He could hear the sound of a motor boat, coming nearer.

As it buzzed past the Murney tower, a sentry with a Kalashnikov and a checkered *keffiyeh* materialized out of the tower's doorway and headed over to the yacht. As he stumbled over a discarded paint bucket, he cursed in Arabic.

Rick and Klaus followed as closely as they dared. From the undergrowth, they watched Alberto Golondrino climb aboard Klaus' yacht.

Before they could react, the yacht and the motor boat had both cast off and were gone, back toward the juncture of the Cataraqui and the St. Lawrence.

"The best laid plans of mice and men..." Rick muttered.

"Gang aft agley. Robbie Burns. I read his poems when I was trying to learn English," Klaus said. "Then I had to re-learn so as not to talk like a Scotsman. Well, we have until tomorrow morning to rest-up and make a new plan, Man."

* * *

CHAPTER TWENTY NINE

L
ike Karla MacTaggart, Alberto Golondrino, aka Iqbal Ghali Ruíz, liked the nine millimetre Parabellum calibre. He was loading some 115 grain hollow-point cartridges into the magazine of his CZ 75 semi-auto when Dieter Gipfel bounded down the stairs into the galley of the Delilah, formerly La Cime du Plaisir.

"You're bubbling over with energy today, Dieter." Inserting the magazine into the gun, he dropped the slide, then carefully lowered the hammer and holstered it, right next to the wallet containing twenty hundred-dollar bills. There were two others similarly stuffed in different pockets of his Tilley pants. "You didn't sleep much last night. Did you have a bit of nose candy for breakfast?"

"Yeah. A little eye-opener. Keeps me sharp." Dieter's pupils were wide and black.

"Well I want you to get a good sleep tonight. Tomorrow will be the big bang. A lot of folks are counting on you and the lads." He shoved a vial of prescription capsules across the table to Dieter. "These are mild – Oxazepam. One or two will cool you out tonight, and be burned-off by the magic hour. This is a fine yacht; it fits our purpose well. It's awfully nice of your dad to lend it to us."

"Well my awfully nice dad reported it stolen two days ago," Dieter snapped. "That's why we had to paint it and change the fucking name. He's a straight-arrow dip-stick."

"Whatever that means," Alberto replied. "Still, disguising the boat was a good idea in any case. How are the lads?"

"They're in the guest rooms over the boat house, chattering away with Abu in Arabic or French. French I know a bit. Not Arabic. He seems to be keeping them under control, and instructing them in the safe handling of Sarin. He's been in charge of that part of it." Dieter stamped about impatiently in the narrow confines of the galley, peered out the port-hole to the boat house and shook his head.

"This craft is two metres too long and a half metre too wide to fit into the boat-house."

"Well, I did the best I could on short notice. Moored here, on the dock beside it, we're pretty-well screened by that weeping willow. The good thing is that it's only twenty minutes from here down river to RMC. The RPG's and ammo stayed snug in the crate at the motel. I'm sure nobody saw us uncovering it and loading it aboard at that hour of the morning. And nobody will think to look for us here, north of the 401."

"Have those four Arabs been well-trained?" Dieter asked. Standing in the galley, he was licking his lips and wiping the sweat off his hands onto his camo trousers.

"*Ojalá.*" It is a Spanish word, meaning 'one hopes'. The expression came from the Moorish occupation of the Iberian peninsula during Islam's glory-days. Literally 'Oh to Allah' or God willing." Alberto elaborated, "Mahmoud Khalid, our Saudi friend whom you met in Playa del Carmen, has recommended all of them. And Abu Tomari met Sayeed Surat, our insider at RMC, when he went to the madrasa in Pakistan. He says he's dedicated to the jihad."

"Are you?" Dieter challenged.

"Why else would I be here, *amigo*, taking these risks?"

"For the same reason I am. I don't give a tweety-bird's twat for your jihad, Alberto, and I suspect you don't either. You <u>are</u> getting well-paid for this operation, and for the coke we brought in."

"And so are you, *muñeco*. It doesn't detract from one's noble cause to be adequately compensated for risk and effort. And a complex operation, brilliantly executed, is a thing of awesome beauty. It will get the attention of the world."

"What's *muñeco* mean?"

"It means cute, attractive, a male doll. You are still attractive to me Dieter. You don't realize, perhaps, how important your presence has been in my life."

Dieter stood, stiff and guarded for a few seconds, then moved closer to the table.

Alberto reached out and grasped the buckle of his wide belt of tooled leather. "I gave you this belt, *muñeco*. Come, stay with me a while. I can help you to relax."

* * *

CHAPTER THIRTY

The two warriors sat in the darkness with their backs to an ancient oak tree, overlooking the Cataraqui River. There had been a light frost in the night, touching the upper leaves. When the sun would arise behind them in an hour, the diamond-droplets would drip down on their necks. By then, it might be all over. They might be dead.

"You ever kill anyone, Rick?"

"No. Came close once when I was a cop. He dropped the rifle just in time. You get a whole lot of legal trouble if you have to shoot someone."

"We're both hunters, Rick. We've been out like this before, at dawn, waiting for the world to wake up; for the action to start."

"Yeah, but it's different taking out one of your own kind. Not only legally different. It's like the difference between a carnivore and a cannibal."

"But it wouldn't bother you a lot if you had to?" Klaus asked.

"I think not. They used to tell us in training that the best scenario would be that nobody gets hurt. The worst is that you get killed and the bad guy gets away. And even the Criminal Code gives us the right to use deadly force to save an innocent life."

"We're counting on that, aren't we?"

"We better hope we get a sympathetic judge, if we're alive to even come to trial. So far, my luck hasn't been terrific on that score," Rick observed.

"Two against six…"

"Seven," Rick said. "Remember, Alberto Golondrino joined them yesterday. You're not getting cold feet now, are you Klaus?"

"No, no. I'm as brave, or as foolhardy as you are. But it would be nice to have some help in this, at an earlier stage."

"We can't. We've already discussed it, Klaus. Noreen and Lucy and the rest – Karla, Victor too – they'll alert Milos Novak, who may be in on the plot. Even if they don't, once the Coast Guard or the Military realize something's afoot, the Kingston Police and the OPP won't be kept out of it. And we both know about governments. They can't act legally until it's too late and the damage is done, and they're prone to shooting up the wrong folks with friendly fire. A pre-emptive strike to neutralize the sons-of-bitches, and we'll call in the cops *pronto*. We agreed on that." Rick tapped his cell phone in his breast pocket for emphasis.

"Don't malign bitches. Treu is one. Just kidding Rick. Two against seven seems about right, when we're the two!"

"Good thinking, Klaus. It was you who spotted the yacht there," he said, gesturing with his rifle barrel down the bank toward the shadow of the boat house below them.

"Well, when it wasn't at the Rideau Marina, nor at the motel, and the crate of ammo was gone, I thought we should search the river, you by vehicle on Highway 15, and I with the canoe."

"With that two horse kicker and bracket, and Treu for ballast, you were motoring right along. I never would have found the thing moored beneath that weeping willow. Well, we're about to teach the weeping willow how to cry."

"That's from a song by Johnny Cash," Klaus said, "about a love he lost. Big River."

"Kind of *a propos*. I've lost a wife, a daughter and a girl-friend. You've lost a wife and have disowned your son. At least you've got a grand-daughter to love you."

"If I survive long enough to raise her. Look, Rick. Morning has broken, like the first morning."

"God, we're lyrical this morning. And the wind is going to pick-up from the south-west. Let's move!"

"*Er starb im Kampf um die Freiheit*," Klaus muttered.

"What?"

"He died in the struggle for freedom. It's on a lot of German tomb-stones."

"Well let's make sure it's the bad guys under them and not us."

* * *

CHAPTER THIRTY ONE

Abu Tomari and the rest of the jihadists slept above the boat house. Of the four new Canadians, two rotated as sentries every two and a half hours.

On board the Delilah, Alberto Golondrino arose before dawn, careful not to wake the snoring Dieter Gipfel. He'd downed enough Oxazepam to drug an elephant, but cocaine addicts could sop-up a truck-load. And if Dieter should overdose and die – so what? He was too erratic to be of much use to them anymore. If he were eliminated, somehow, there would be more of the final pay-off for Alberto, so long as the mission was completed.

As the sky atop the wooded ridge grew brighter, Alberto gave a low whistle and a *Salaam* to the sentry on the roof of the boat house. The wave of his camouflaged arm let the sentry see his CZ. It didn't hurt to let the troops know that the general was armed and alert. Frosted ferns on the path leading uphill brushed the bottoms of his Tilley pants. Frost, in May! Only in Canada, or perhaps in fucking Finland.

When Alberto came to where the second sentry should be, he could not see him at first. He whistled the two note signal, killdeer. All he heard was a moan.

Drawing his pistol, he approached like a jaguar stalking a javelina. He found the sentry on his belly, keffiyeh binding his wrists behind him, a short cord around his ankles, flexing them up to his bum and a piece of duct tape over his mouth. The AK-47 lay on the ground beside him, with a green stick driven into the barrel and broken off at the muzzle.

"It serves you right for falling asleep on the job," Alberto said in Arabic as he untied him. "How many are there, and where did they go?"

"Just two. One is an old guy. Both *kefirs.*" It was the Arabic word for unbeliever or infidel. "They were heading toward the yacht."

"You get down there and wake the others. Get yourself re-armed and guard the boat. I'll scout around here a while before I join you. We have to get out of here, quickly, but don't leave without me."

"God is great," the man said as he left.

Yes, but if you run into a hail of bullets, I'm going to take my exit another way, Alberto thought. Aloud, he agreed. "God is great."

* * *

CHAPTER
THIRTY TWO

The frost was melting with the rising sun. It was wet, slow work for Rick to creep along the path, through the dripping foliage, to try to get to the Delilah and disable the craft.

Klaus was going after the sentry on the roof of the boat house. There was an iron ladder up the outside of the structure. With a sling fastened to the twelve gauge, he could climb using both hands. The nagging pain in his left knee from osteoarthritis had faded to a mere whisper now.

A handgun started popping away up on the embankment, where they had left the first sentry. Slugs splintered the wooden building around Klaus. He couldn't let go of the ladder to get at his shotgun, and the sentry would be on full alert now.

Klaus could hear shouts from inside the boat house. The bullets must have penetrated the upper story guest rooms. Maybe the odds were a bit better now. Maybe some of the enemy would be disabled by that wild guy upon the hillside.

Klaus looked up over the rim of the roof and found himself staring down the muzzle of an AK-47.

* * *

Rick had caught a glimpse of Alberto Golondrino with his CZ nine millimetre, before he vanished behind some rocks and brush, presumably to re-load. Rick's rifle was pointed back that way. Just one clear shot… The rising sun came searing through his scope, blinding him for a moment.

As he squirmed around, blinking, a rifle round whunked into the earth where he'd been lying an instant before. He rolled to one side, and put himself behind a bush, shielding him from the yacht, for that was where the shot had come from. A bush, however, is only penetrable cover.

In a cyclone of events, seemingly slowed down by his panicked brain, Rick could see a gut-wrenching scenario unfolding. Dieter, aboard the yacht, was steadying himself against the rail and peering through the Summit Industry scope of his .243, trying to get another shot at Rick. To Dieter's right, on the boat house roof, the sentry, momentarily distracted by Dieter's shot, was preparing to blow Dieter's father's head off. Klaus yelled Dieter's name.

It was not a difficult shot for Rick to make from a prone position at sixty metres. His slug hit the receiver of the Kalashnikov and knocked the sentry sprawling.

Klaus scrambled up onto the roof. The sentry lay stunned, the wind knocked out of him. He'd be no problem for a while. To make his body a smaller target, Klaus assumed a sitting position, shotgun unslung and pointing at Dieter.

Rick, too, now had his cross-hairs centred on Dieter's chest, waiting to see any sign of an imminent shot.

Only thirty metres separated father and son. The shotgun had rifled slugs alternating with buckshot in the magazine.

"Give it up, Dieter!" Klaus called.

Dieter raised his head from the stock of the rifle. "No! You give it up, Old Man. I might just let you live if you fuck off right now and mind your own business. Put the gun down, Dad!"

Klaus' voice floated back to Rick's ears, filled with an infinite sadness. "I'm afraid I can not, Son. I'm sorry."

Dieter's cheek went back to the gun stock.

Rick's finger tightened on the trigger of his.308.

Two shots rang out from the hillside. One of them tore into the cabin of the yacht and smashed the compass. The other seared along Dieter's forearm and hit him in the thigh. He fired, but the shot went wild. Then he crawled back into the cabin of the vessel, leaving a trail of blood.

Pushing the safety back on his rifle, Rick dropped the hinged magazine and inserted a fresh cartridge. Always re-load when you have the opportunity, he'd learned. He crawled to a dogwood bush that gave him some protection from the sun's glare and scanned the wooded slope, looking for Golondrino.

Instead he saw Karla MacTaggart, his former mother-in-law, her Browning HiPower in her hands, seated on the ground with both arms braced on her knees. It was she who had shot Dieter! Where was Golondrino?

With shouts in Arabic that God is great, Abu Tomari and three new-Canadian terrorists burst out of the boat house with rifles and quickly found cover in the bushes and boulders behind it. They did not realize that Klaus was still up on the roof, his shotgun ready, and he could see at least two of the four men.

What Klaus did not know was that the stunned sentry on the roof had re-gained his breath, moved in behind him with his disabled rifle, and was preparing to bash him on the head with it.

Rick was about ready to put the terrorist down permanently when the man burst into flames. With a scream, he dropped the rifle and ran off the front of the boat house roof. He sizzled as he hit the river.

Klaus was cut in the shoulder by a piece of flying glass that imbedded itself into his flesh.

Omar Tomari strode around the side of the boat house. He gave Rick a grin and thumbs-up. Extracting a fresh naphtha-based Molotov cocktail from his haversack, he moved toward the yacht. He had his Bic lighter in the other hand.

"Omar! No!" Rick shouted and stood up. "There's nerve gas aboard. You can't risk it!"

Omar stood there immobilized, looking at Rick, and then looking past him, His eyes widened.

Like a statue, Rick stood, uncomprehending. As he started to crouch and whirl around, he heard the sound of flesh hitting flesh.

Lucy Lam lay sprawled on the ground, next to Alberto Golondrino. His CZ had been knocked out of his hand by her kick. She'd run down the hill at full stride and hit him in the back with both feet as she flung herself through space. Lucy had never tried that move before. She'd seen it in a Kung Fu movie. The actors must have had a softer place to land than the rocky shore of the Cataraqui River.

As Abu and his men commenced firing, things got even more interesting and everyone scrambled for cover. Bullets whizzed about like high-velocity hornets and the occasional naphtha bomb burst its glass container to flying shards, but no one seemed to get badly hurt.

Rick crawled again the few paces to where Lucy was lying.

"Y'all look like a side-winder, pardner," she said to him.

"I was going to ask 'Are you all right?' like they always do in the movies, but I see you are. Yeah. I've been snaking around on my belly all morning. Every time I stand up, someone tries to kill me. Thanks, eh. Where's Golondrino?"

"I don't know. I guess he crawled off. I would, if I were him, wouldn't you?"

"Lucy, stay here between these two boulders. I'm going to sneak through that boat house and try to get a fix on Abu Tomari."

"Rick don't...." she started to say, but he was gone.

* * *

It was what they called a Mexican stand-off.

Rick had left his rifle in the boat house. There was a door on one side, but only a window on the other. He still had his .45 when he circled around in the bush and came upon Abu Tomari, clutching a Kalashnikov. They were eight metres apart, both kneeling, facing each other.

Rick knew he could draw and fire in one third of a second; about the same time it would take for Abu to bring the assault rifle to bear on him.

"Please don't kill my son," Omar had pleaded with him. That made him hesitate. And that hesitation could get him killed.

Abu, too, seemed to hesitate. Both men could hear the engine of the Delilah start up. Neither looked. They could hear that the yacht was moving south, past the boat house. They would soon be visible to anyone who was on board.

The tension was as taut as a guitar string about to snap.

Just as Rick was about to draw and fire in one smooth movement, as he'd done a thousand times before, the voice of Milos Novak came from behind him.

"Rick. It's under control. Stay calm. It's all right. Be cool."

Be cool. The Czech creep was in on the plot! But he probably had a gun pointed at Rick's back. And Abu Tomari had not dropped his AK-47.

Then Lucy screamed from her hiding place; an unintelligible wail of terror.

Abu raised the Kalashnikov and turned toward the yacht. Dieter was standing beside the cabin, a bazooka on his shoulder, aiming at them. He was about to take them out all at once with an RPG!

Eight of the fifteen bullets Abu sent in a burst hit Dieter. The bazooka fell at his feet as his life's blood ran out of his crumpled body around it.

Alberto Golondrino was at the helm, heading down river toward the Royal Military College!

* * *

CHAPTER THIRTY THREE

Alberto Golondrino could still pull it off! With the others out of the way, the final payment would be made to him alone.

Once beyond the bend in the river, approaching the Highway 401 bridge that crossed it, he reduced his speed and strapped the wheel with the two rubber bands there for the purpose. The cabin had been spattered with rifle rounds, the compass and windshield cracked, but the yacht was still functional.

After lowering the radio aerial so he could get the craft under both of the bridges between him and RMC, he unceremoniously dumped Dieter's perforated, bloody body into the river. The bazooka, he kept. He had one other. This was for back up only. With a rag, he wiped the blood off the black weapon and checked to be sure it was loaded and ready to fire.

Back in the cabin, Alberto made a minor adjustment with the rubber straps and inspected the other bazooka, a gray one. This contained the rocket with the Sarin.

Even if it was still too early for the ceremony, enough people would be up and about to get a lungful of the vapour as it spread. The breeze from the south-west was freshening. Perfect. The head honchos at al-Qaida would be impressed. No doubt even Osama bin Laden himself would know, though he was, at the moment, keeping a very low profile.

With every possibility anticipated and his armament verified and ready, he revved the engine and sped down river toward RMC. Canada's future Admirals, Generals and Air Marshals would not live to see their youthful pretensions realized.

* * *

Once clear of the LaSalle Causeway at Highway Two, Alberto's way was unhampered to get into position for the shot. He could see a crimson "poker-run" speed boat moving out from beside the dock of the Wolfe Island Ferry.

This was to pick him up, right after the deed, and buzz him right across Lake Ontario to Oswego, New York. A safe house awaited him there. He'd hunker down for a few days, call up another boat at his disposal, and go back to Canada, landing at Picton. The *Yanquis* were much more vigilant about security than the Canadians since 9-11. He'd spend as brief a time as possible in the U.S.

As Alberto swung the yacht around, then put the twin screws into neutral, he was surprised how sparse the boat traffic was for a week-end. Apart from the Wolfe Islander II, churning back toward Kingston, and his red escape speed boat moving closer, there was only a small, slow, fishing boat with three guys in it.

Stepping out onto the deck with the gray weapon, Alberto could see the break in the trees just to the left of the Martello Tower of Fort Frederick. He shouldered the bazooka. From here, he could plop that Sarin-filled grenade right into the middle of the parade square of the Royal Military College.

A rifle ball, completely shattering the cabin's windshield, interrupted him.

It had come from the fishing boat, now only fifty metres away. A cloud of white smoke was drifting across the gentle waves.

Scrambling for cover, Alberto put the gray weapon onto the rack and grabbed the black one. Through the sights, he could see an Oriental at the stern, and two Fort Henry guards with antique 18th century, guardsman rifles. They thought they could stop him with those chunks of *mierda*?

He took aim, ready to blow them to the Hell reserved for infidels. At that range, he couldn't miss. With only his right eye and ear exposed, those guys were history.

With cool precision, he squeezed the trigger of the black bazooka.

* * *

CHAPTER THIRTY FOUR

Victor Lam had quietly recruited two of his best student-cadets to the cause. They had summer jobs as Fort Henry guards and could get their hands on rifles, albeit ancient ones.

He'd considered taking along some of the naphtha grenades he'd made, but explosions around Sarin would not be a good idea. He'd given them all to his sister, Lucy, to pass out to the others, as needed.

When he'd set out before dawn in the small craft, he had explained to the cadets that their presence was only a precaution. He didn't know for sure if there <u>was</u> to be an attack on RMC, or if Sarin was involved, or if Lucy, Karla, Noreen and Omar would be able to stop the bad guys before they left their berth up river. And Rick Amyotte was what they call a loose cannon. In China, a land he'd never seen, he would probably be labeled a berserk dragon.

I suppose that's what I am too, he thought as they waited for dawn to break in the boat slip beside the Tim Horton's Donut Shop.

When it did, the day seemed fresh and bright – perfect for a killing. He and his two eager recruits moved off shore and pretended to be trolling for muskies.

Two hours later, Victor recognized La Cime du Plaisir, coming down-river into the lake. Using binoculars, he could see the new-paint job, the stellated window, and Alberto Golondrino at the helm.

The Jihadist terrorists had not been stopped. Victor and two kids with archaic muskets were all that stood between this perfect day and a colossal tragedy!

"Wait until someone comes out on deck before you make your shot," he advised. "You have to knock him into the lake, with his weapon, for there may be others on board. But you can't let him shoot toward the College."

"Of course not," one replied. "It's our Alma Mater, eh?'

When Alberto came on deck with the bazooka, it was the guy in the bow who took the first shot. Muskets are not terribly accurate, and a small boat in waves, even gentle ones, is not a stable shooting platform.

After the shot, they were astonished at how quickly Golondrino got back under cover. Seconds later, a black bazooka had its muzzle pointing at their tiny craft.

Victor gunned the motor as the second cadet tried to shoot.

He held back, for their own boat was now lurching and swerving.

The black rocket-launcher belched smoke. A grenade plopped feebly into the lake between them and the yacht. It was a squib round!

* * *

Alberto didn't know whether to curse in Spanish or Arabic. There was an AK-47 in the gun rack, but the magazine was removed. Where in hell had that little useless armadillo Dieter hid it? Can't ask him now, he thought.

162

Opening the ammo crate, the first thing he found was a fresh RPG round. Well, maybe this one would work.

"Pendejo-kefirs," he muttered in Spanish and Arabic as he inserted the round and prepared to fire again. Even swerving, that boat was momentarily stopped at the apex of each zig and zag. His finger took up the slack on the electronic ignition trigger and he waited. At exactly the right moment, with the cross-hairs on the middle of the boat, centered on the second cadet, Alberto Golondrino, aka Iqbal Ghali Ruíz, once again fired off an RPG.

That was the last look he had, or would ever have. The squib round, altered by Rick and Klaus, had left the base of the rocket stuck in the barrel. The fresh grenade, on striking it, exploded with such violence it tore the cabin of the Delilah and Iqbal Ghali Ruíz, to shreds.

"Oh God, no!" Victor exclaimed, watching the vapour drifting on the wind. "There's Sarin on board, and it's heading right toward RMC!"

* * *

The crimson speed boat hesitated after the explosion, waiting to see if there would be any survivors to extricate from the burning hull. When none appeared, it turned to flee through the Gap between the Islands Wolfe and Amherst.

It didn't make it. A flotilla of armed craft, Coast Guard, OPP and Canadian Navy which had been lurking behind Garden and Simcoe Islands emerged to block the escape. More were coming from behind Cedar Island in the St. Lawrence and more from Kingston itself.

The men in the crimson craft raised their arms in surrender.

Meanwhile, Victor Lam and the two cadets watched the cloud of smoke filtering through the trees on the shoreline, right toward their College.

* * *

CHAPTER
THIRTY FIVE

D r. Lucy Lam was occupied trying to extricate a chunk of glass out of the shoulder of Klaus Gipfel. She was using Rick's hunting knife, the blade sterilized with naphtha gas, ignited by a BIC lighter. They were down on the dock beside the boat house, where the yacht had been moored.

Rick was sitting on a boulder, staring suspiciously at Abu Tomari.

His father, Omar, also seemed less than completely forgiving. He was standing, erect and rigid, except for a noticeable tremor in his hands. A naphtha grenade slipped out of one and shattered at his feet. He stared down, uncomprehending, puzzled, in shock. Just as Omar started to faint – before Rick could move – Noreen moved in to support him. She guided him to a bench under a sugar maple. Rick was surprised to see that she, too, had a haversack full of naphtha grenades. He'd never thought of Noreen as a warrior before.

"Lucy Lam!" Milos Novak called out. "Can you get over here? I've got your brother, Victor on the radio. Apparently our guys scooped him and a couple of cadets out of the lake. Can you clarify for us? He's raving about a cloud of nerve gas over RMC."

"I'll tend to Klaus," Karla told Lucy. "You go talk to your brother."

"And talk in English, not Chinese," Milos instructed as he handed the speaker and head set to Lucy. "We need to hear what you say."

"Did we get him?" Abu called out.

"Yeah. Iqbal Ghali Ruíz managed to blow himself up, together with Klaus' boat."

"It's not my boat," Klaus said. "I reported it stolen. It's insured for three-quarters of a million bucks."

"Keep still," Karla instructed him. "I've almost got it. Now this is going to hurt," she said as she flicked the piece of glass out with the knife tip, "didn't it?"

"Am I in safe hands with you, Gentle Lady?"

"Certified in first aid by the St John's Ambulance," Karla replied.

"And you're one hell of a shot with that Browning," Klaus marveled.

"Well, I missed with the first shot; got lucky with the second."

"Modest too."

"Abu!" Lucy said. "Victor's still worried about poison gas or something down there."

"Tell him there is no Sarin! The RPG grenade was armed with poison all right. It was gas-line-antifreeze. As long as no one drinks it, it's harmless. I ought to know. I made it up myself."

"Sorry to spoil your Lone Ranger and Tonto caper, Rick," Noreen called out from under the maple. She still had her arm around Omar, though he was looking a lot better. "Have you figured it out yet, or are you as thick as maple fudge?"

"All right, already," Rick said. "Why did nobody try to warn me and Klaus?"

Lucy handed the radio back to Milos, who spoke briefly into it and broke contact.

"No one did, Rick," Milos explained, "because we all know you. You are brave, capable, and determined."

"You are also arrogant and a drunk," Noreen added.

"Was," Rick replied. "Was a drunk. I'm sober now."

"For how long, Rick? Milos asked.

"For today, at least." He turned to Abu. "When did you turn against the jihad?"

"After I came back from the madrasa in Pakistan. Remember, I was just a confused kid then, not even sure of my sexuality. Well now I am. I've come out."

"And Islam condemns homosexuality," Rick said. "Were you in love with Dieter?"

"Was," Abu replied. "After he shot that guy at Tulum, I fell quickly out of love. I also had a brief crush on Alberto, until I realized what a psychopath he is."

"Was," Rick repeated. "He blew himself up, we just learned."

"The Lord moves in a mysterious way," Noreen put in.

She would say that, Rick thought. "So correct me if I'm wrong, but here is my take on this. Abu, you learned that your religion would reject you. You also made contact with Muslim fanatics who are out to destroy anything and anyone contrary to their narrow views. You kept under cover as a good Muslim and chance made you the Case Management Officer of Dieter Gipfel while he was in prison for shooting your Mom."

"Well, not entirely chance. I maneuvered myself into that position. I'd met Sergeant Novak and we agreed that I might be able to uncover a drug organization by befriending Dieter. I didn't count on falling in love. When I did, and when I found out he was dealing with not only druggers but Islamist terrorists, I played along, thinking I could keep him from doing harm. Even after he shot that guy in Mexico, I had to pretend."

"By then, Rick, we had too much invested," Milos said. "We wanted the whole organization – *narcotraficantes* and jihadists combined. When you moved in on your own, we were afraid you'd screw up our trap."

"The sudden wealth of you two was not ill-gotten?"

"What we were doing was both important and dangerous," Abu explained. "CSIS and the RCMP have special funds for operatives like us."

Lucy said, "When Noreen walked out on you, Rick, I went with her. You and I both knew she'd tell Milos what we knew. I went too, mainly to try to protect you and Klaus from two things."

"Two things? One was to stop us from messing up the operation. The other?"

"To keep you from getting killed, of course," Lucy said. "I convinced Milos that you could be useful in your own way, and we'd keep you under surveillance the whole time. Between me, Karla, Noreen, Omar and Milos, we had enough bodies for twice round-the-clock coverage."

"It was not my idea," Milos explained, "to have you civilians in on the final raid. But Karla had tailed you and found out that the boat was here. We didn't know. You found it first. Karla found you, told us, then insisted that she and the rest be in on the raid."

"Call me the Lone Ranger," Rick said, "but I sure appreciate the help. Thank you."

"You are amazing," Klaus said to Karla. His wound was all neatly bandaged and he was putting on his army-surplus camo-shirt with epaulets. "You all are," he added.

"And Victor? What was he doing down at the mouth of the river?" Rick asked.

"My brother is a lot like you, Rick," Lucy said. "He admires you." The warm sun bronzed the skin of her arms. She still had dirt on her elbows from her fall. To Rick, she was beautiful.

"He's like me in that he and a couple of cadets went out as back up for the Army, Navy, Coast Guard and three police forces? He doesn't trust governments either? For sure, Victor is half-way to being a macho-cowboy-paranoid like Klaus and me!"

"Don't encourage him, Lucy," Noreen said dryly. "Soon he'll have Victor beating a drum and running naked through the trees with him and Klaus."

Rick didn't even respond. He just grinned. It was going to be a beautiful day.

* * *

CHAPTER
THIRTY SIX

T he canoe cleaved a golden vee across the placid bosom of the lake. The paddle rose and fell in a steady rhythm, droplets cascading like unstrung pearls on the forward stroke. Tendrils of mist lurked in the shadows where the sun would not find them for another hour.

Rick felt a kinship with his forebears, the *Voyageurs*, the *Coureurs-de-bois*. Trying not to clunk the paddle on the canoe, he swung the craft around and back-paddled a bit to stop its forward momentum.

"Cast over there, beside those lily pads," he commanded.

Her arm rose up vertical. Careful with the back swing, she cast forward. The lure plopped like a frog jumping off a water-lily. Her hair gleamed flaxen in the morning sun.

Rick saw her beauty and felt a warm glow of love.

"*Qu' il reste là bas quelques moments,*" he said.

"How come you talk to me so much in French?" Mona asked him.

"How come you say 'how come', when 'why' is shorter and simpler? So you won't forget it, that's why. You spent the first five years of your life in Montreal. In Ontario, you're surrounded by English. Just remember the language you learned at your mother's knee."

"*Je me souviens*," Mona replied. " 'I remember'. It's on the Quebec license plates. "But are we out here for a language lesson Uncle Rick, or to fish?"

"Good point. Give the lure a twitch or two and wait."

Mona did. Her rod tip arched down to touch the water's surface.

"Wait until he has a good hold on it, then hit him!" Rick said.

"Hit him? How?"

"Jerk the rod back to set the hook! Then reel in slowly."

She did. Line peeled out against the drag as the bass fought for the cover of the weeds.

Rick was back-paddling frantically for deeper water as the fish surfaced and tail-walked, trying to shake the hook. Twice more it searched for depth, than tried the same aerial leap, each time a bit weaker.

Ten minutes later, Rick netted the monster bass, bonked it with a piece of broken oar handle he kept for that purpose, and put it on a stringer. "There is your lunch," he said to Mona.

"Are you going to stay with us for lunch, Uncle Rick? Aunt Karla will be back with Grandpa Klaus by then. She'll cook it for us. There's enough for all of us. We can have blueberry pie for dessert, too!"

"No. It's tempting, though. I'll stay another time. I have to meet Lucy for lunch down in Kingston."

"If I catch another fish, you could take it with you and cook it for her for dinner. I bet she'd like that, her."

Rick noted that Mona still had a French way of talking, even in English. "Yes, I'm sure she would. Let's try up there by those reeds, in the shadow of the cliff."

"Grandpa Klaus and Aunt Karla are going to get married, and I'm to be the ring-bearer, on a white satin cushion."

"Yes, I heard that. I'll be there." He didn't ask her if she'd be on the cushion, or the rings.

"How did you meet Aunt Karla, Rick? You knew her before even Grandpa."

"She and I came from the same town in Northern Quebec. Then she became my mother-in-law."

"Mother-in-law?"

"Yes. She is Noreen's mother. I was married to Noreen. Now I'm not. Things like that happen, sometimes, Mona."

"And now you're with Lucy, and Noreen is with Omar Tomari, I think. This is more confusing than a game of chess! Are you going to marry with Lucy?"

Rick slowed the canoe again. "Cast over there, at the edge of the shade." And your Mom has gone to heaven and your Daddy's gone to hell, Rick thought. Poor little creature.

"Well, are you?" Mona said as she cast. "People do, you know."

"And sometimes it turns out wrong."

"But not always, Uncle Rick. You have to take a chance. Oh, I think I've got another strike!"

* * *

CHAPTER
THIRTY SEVEN

"**G**ood swing, Lucy," Rick said. They were at the Kingston Trap and Skeet Club. Rick was giving her a private lesson in shotgun technique.

"But I missed!"

"Doesn't matter. Your move was right. So was your follow-through. Let's try it again. This time, do the same thing, but see a bit more daylight between your front bead and the target before you press the trigger."

Lucy smashed the clay disc with the next shot.

"I could become addicted to this," she exclaimed. "But don't expect me to go hunting with you. Dead clay-birds I don't mind. You get the feathered ones, I'll stay home."

"Clear enough. Let's move to the next station. The angle is greater. Same move, more lead."

She was doing it again – staking out her parameters. Rick both admired and hated that characteristic. She was a lot like he was. There were limits beyond which he wouldn't go as well. They were just different than her limits. Maybe it's something in the air around the Quebec mining town where they each had their roots.

With the next box of shells, Lucy hit fourteen out of twenty-five targets.

"I think you're ready to try a round of Sporting Clays," Rick said. "Are you free on Sunday morning?"

"Could be. Can I use this gun?" It was an old Beretta twelve-gauge semi-auto with a shortened stock. Rick had enlarged the gas vent in the barrel so that it functioned flawlessly with light, one-ounce loads.

"Sure. It's yours, once your Possession and Acquisition License comes through."

"Thank you, Rick. Are you trying to bribe me with this gift so that you can have your way with me?"

"Most definitely. And you can have your way with me."

"Offer accepted. Your place or mine?" she asked smiling.

* * *

Sitting on the wolf-skin on her piano bench, Lucy played Beethoven's Moonlight Sonata. She only had to glance at the music occasionally. Her brother, Victor, had it, and a hundred other bits of music by long-dead Europeans, memorized perfectly.

Rick sat in an armchair, next to the artificial fire-place, with its flames springing out of the gas-jets in the artificial logs, nursing a drink. When she finished, he stood up, went and kissed her on the neck and said, "That was beautiful. Thank you for that, Lucy."

"You're welcome. Want some?" She was raising a half-full bottle of Riesling out of an ice-bucket.

"No, I'll stick to grape-juice and soda-water, for today." He went back to the arm chair. "I've been thinking…"

"That's good, Rick," she said as she settled onto the sofa. "You stop thinking, you're either dead or into a dementia. About what?"

"The pattern of things. Fate. Destiny."

"Mmm. Profound. You're not just a macho lover, you're a philosopher. Enlighten me, please."

"It was something Mona said to me. She's only six, 'going on seven' as she's quick to add, but she made me think of all the connections we've made – a lot of them through our parents' home town. I'm arranging for Klaus and me to go there this fall to hunt moose. The licenses would be more expensive than hunting in Ontario, but there are some Amyottes we can stay with. My uncle will be our guide."

"Oh. You're re-visiting your roots. That's nice."

"But that's not all I've been thinking. If Karla's Dad and my Dad hadn't discovered gold, and if Karla hadn't been best friends with your Mom, then none of us would be in South Eastern Ontario. We would never have met."

"Oh, we might have. You would be a cop with the Sureté du Québec, and I'd be proprietress of a Chinese restaurant and a laundry. We might have met."

"We'd be different people than we are, Lucy."

"I know. If Golondrino hadn't poisoned your daughter, Tanya, you and Noreen would not have contacted me in toxicology. Golondrino led you to Dieter Gipfel, who led you to his father, Klaus, and Abu Tomari, and hence Omar. Then add in Mona, and my brother, Victor, and Milos Novak. At least you got Golondrino, the guy who murdered Tanya. How does Noreen feel about that?"

"Well, revenge is never as sweet as you think it will be. We don't know why Golondrino poisoned Tanya, or if he really wanted her dead. He must have known about 9-11, so it was willful negligence, probably for reasons of sexual exploitation, if not murder. But no one has captured Osama Bin Laden yet, the main architect of that attack. At least we've eliminated Dieter and Golondrino, two very evil psychopaths. We're happy to be alive, of course. But Klaus lost a son in that affair."

"Dieter was already lost. He was ready to shoot his own father when Karla dinged him with her pistol and Abu showed his true colours by terminating him for good. And you stopped a terrorist attack on RMC and rounded-up a bunch of Islamic fanatics."

"Not 'you.' 'We'. And Klaus has connected with Karla and found Mona, his grand-daughter. Fate?"

"You know the story of the horse-shoe nail, Rick?"

"Because of a nail, a shoe was lost; because of a shoe, a rider was lost; because of a rider, a message was lost and so on."

"Exactly. It's the way life is. A butterfly flaps its wings in Hong Kong and an earthquake results in Los Angeles. I know you don't have much, or any religious faith, Rick. So this isn't by God's great plan?"

"No. Noreen would think so. I don't."

"Then it's just a peculiar concatenation of events and individuals that has connected us."

"Concatenation?"

"From the Latin for chain. A linked series. There is no sense to it, Rick. It's random; chance."

"You don't think we are meant for each other, you and I?" he asked.

"I don't believe in pre-destination. Neither do you – you ninny. Otherwise, we'd have no free choice at all. Rick, you are strong, and brave, and handsome, and intelligent and loving...."

"You left out bi-lingual and sober, at least for today. But you're quadra-lingual, so it doesn't count for much. And I can't even play a musical instrument."

"Don't put yourself down, Rick."

"I thought I detected a 'but' in there – a major reservation."

Lucy nodded. "There is a 'but.' Just because this concatenation brought us together doesn't mean it's love eternal. We're quite different people. We share in a lot, and I feel privileged to be part of your life, but I can't be just like you want me to be. You love the country; the bush, the wilderness. I'm a city woman. You shoot guns. You kill things. I'm a doctor, I save lives, where I can. I think it can't work, Rick. It can't." She started to cry.

"Don't you love me, Lucy?"

"Yes, I do, goddamn it. It's just the practical part of it. I've got my career, my profession…"

"I'd never try to interfere with that. It's part of you. But how can you live in the city? It's so crowded, polluted, crime-ridden."

"Think about that last, Rick. Every major action to stop the bad guys took place outside the city!"

"All right. You'll concede crowded and polluted?"

"Yes. And the country is isolated and inconvenient, especially if I have to get to the Hospital in a hurry."

"It's a stand-off. So I'm going to throw in two more things on my side. One is, I've put in an offer on a house on a lake on the Bedford Road, just north-east of Sydenham. From there, you could be to the Hospital in half an hour, less if it's not rush hour. With a cell phone, you could be in touch all the way. Speaker head-set, of course. I still think like a cop. Safety first."

"That's it? You mentioned two things. The cell phone is the second?"

"No. All that was the first." Rick went to the sofa and sat down beside her. "The second is that I adore you. I'm determined to make our relationship work. I'll take you on any terms you want, Lucy. Of course I'll bargain for what I want. But you'll always win. Just so long as you love me. That's all I ask."

"And you've been sober for seven months."

"Eight. I'm stubborn, dedicated. But I can be flexible too."

"Is this a proposal? I'm not ready to marry you, Rick. Maybe I never will be."

"Then call it a proposition. Move into my new house with me, Lucy. Try it for six months. Then we can re-evaluate."

"Can we have a dog?"

"One of Treu's nephews or nieces. Klaus says the litter is due next week. Seven weeks from then, we get a pup. And puppies are cute."

"Very cute," she admitted. "I'd prefer a niece."

"So would I. They're..."

"I know. Easier to manage. Will you stay here, for tonight, you macho, stubborn, brave, loyal, persuasive...."

"Don't forget loving."

"No. That's the head of the list," Lucy said. "It goes without saying it."

∾ The End ∾

Made in the USA
Charleston, SC
04 March 2015